PONG

A Week with
the Bottle Rabbit

Bernard McCabe

Illustrated by Axel Scheffler

FIBRE & FIBRE

First published in paperback in Great Britain
by Fibre & Fibre, 1997

Published by
Fibre & Fibre
Knowbury Old Farm
Snitton
Ludlow
Shropshire
SY8 3JZ

Distributed by Merlin Unwin Books, Palmers House,
7 Corve Street, Ludlow, Shropshire SY8 1DB

The author asserts his moral right to be identified as
the author of this work.

Typeset in Palatino by Merlin Unwin Books, Ludlow.

ISBN 0 9530248 0 6

Printed in Great Britain by Redwood Books,
Trowbridge, Wiltshire.

Contents

For all those grandchildren
And remembering Stephen

Ken's Merry Pranks

It was a warm Wednesday morning. In the glade, bees buzzed quietly, sheep meekly baa-ed, and silent hedge-hogs went about their silent business. Fred and Charlie's heavy wooden cart, on the other hand, was thumping and creaking through the forest, loaded with wooden mallets; the two great Clydesdales were off on a haulage job. The Bottle Rabbit had waved them goodbye, and he was now sitting in the morning sun on his favourite bench outside their cabin. What a friendly, interesting, and nice-looking young animal he was, with that taut woolly body of his, those comfort-able ears and paws, that kindly expression, and - in his front pocket - that extraordinary Magic Bottle, small, green, mysterious.

Perhaps because it was the beginning of the week (as is well-known, the Forest week always begins on a Wednesday), the rabbit took out his Bottle and looked carefully again at the words inscribed round its neck:

> *This Truth ever bear in Mind,*
> *I'm only useful to the Kind.*

It was an important warning and the rabbit knew all too well that at different times in the past bad animals had ignored it. Using various tricks, they'd got the Magic Bottle away from him, only to find it was no use to them at all, simply wouldn't work. The rabbit, though, had been given the Bottle as a Kindness Prize

1

in the first place, and it always did what he asked of it. At this moment, as it happened, he was feeling hungry (he'd missed breakfast). So he uncorked the Bottle, held it up, as always high over his head, and pongled twice, 'Pongle, Pongle'. Within a minute or two, plop; down thumped a round of delicious sandwiches wrapped in a newly-laundered white napkin; it was egg-and-cress this time, one of his favourites, with a little pot of fresh mayonnaise and a small silver knife.

The rabbit smiled happily as this tasty feast arrived, and had just begun to tuck in when there came a rustling and grunting from behind a hedge, then a rough scuffling; and a large pig, whom he knew very well, came trotting up.

'Why, hullo Ken. How lovely to see you,' he said. Ken the Pig, looking very smart in bottle-green mountain-suit and alpine hat with chamois brush, immediately held out a Teak Box.

'Look after this for me, would you old man?' The rabbit blinked at the Teak Box and took it in his paws. It was heavy.

Ken was smiling at him in his fat way and settling down on the bench for a chat, when firm footsteps and the sound of a rumbling wheel charged the pig's face with concern. To the Bottle Rabbit's astonishment Ken now threw himself with a scrunch full-length into the tall grasses growing near the cabin-door.

'You haven't seen me,' the pig grunted, small eyes glittering through the green.

'But I have seen you, Ken. And anyone else could see you, too' began the Bottle Rabbit, puzzled. But he stopped short when Ken put a warning trotter to his lips.

'Not a word,' hissed the pig.

At that moment a cheerful, harmless badger in over-alls plodded past, pushing a wooden wheelbarrow full of early cabbage.

'Hullo, there,' he said to the rabbit, and 'Hullo Ken,' he added, glancing down. 'Having a little rest Ken? Cheers.'

As this badger plodded on, Ken scrambled out of the flattened grass, sweat pouring down his big pig's head. He took out a red-spotted handkerchief and mopped his brow.

'Phew. A false alarm,' he said, and grinned.

'How do you mean, alarm?' said the puzzled rabbit.

'I mean I thought I'd had it that time.'

'Had what, Ken? What's the matter?

'Matter?' the pig shook his head. 'Nothing at all. Nothing, old man. I just thought it was somebody else.' Ken shook his head again. 'The truth is there is some-body after me. It's this blasted beaver, old man. Follows me about, keeps following me about. He badgers me.'

'What for?'

'*I* don't know, do I? He keeps on hissing and moaning about the 90p I owe him.'

'90p? Is that all?'

'Well, it's 19.90, actually, if you want to be narrow-minded about it. I say, BR, you wouldn't mind letting me have a bite of that lovely great sandwich of yours, would you? I missed breakfast this morning.'

The Bottle Rabbit handed a half-sandwich over and the pig gobbled it down at one go. The rabbit smiled and handed him another, which went the same way.

'Very tasty. Very nice. Just the job.' Ken flicked a few crumbs from his bright yellow waistcoat and beamed cheerfully. 'I don't suppose you could rise to a nice cold bottle of beer to wash that lot down with, old man?'

'Come on, Ken, you know my Magic Bottle only does fizzy drinks and tea and things like that.' Ken groaned comically,

'Oh yes, of course, yes, deary me yes. Make mine a lemonade then'.

The Bottle Rabbit smiled again, did a single pongle, and quite soon a large ice-cold bottle of that delicious beverage plopped down beside them.

The rabbit couldn't help noticing that as he drained his lemonade, Ken kept glancing at him from the corner of his little pig-eyes. Now Ken's tail was beginning to wiggle - always a sign that some scheme was coming up.

'I say, old man, 'said the big pig, 'are you up to doing me a small favour? Between pals?'

'What is it this time, Ken?' asked the rabbit warily.

'It's just this Teak Box, old man, just a Teak Box. But there's a Lamb coming along to collect it and he's bringing me his old purse in exchange. I'm doing him a big favour as a matter of fact.' The Bottle Rabbit sighed.

'Why can't you give this Teak Box to the Lamb yourself, Ken?'

'Well', the pig's tail wiggled faster, 'I've got to go to the Post Office to pick up some poems.' He paused. 'Poems? What am I saying? I mean some parcels. And I told the Lamb I'd meet him here in the Beech Grove. Come on Bottle Rabbit. Be a pal. Be a sport. All you've got to do is collect this old purse of his and hand him his Teak Box.' The Bottle Rabbit looked uncertain.

'What's in the Box, Ken?'

'In the Teak Box? Just some machinery for making things. Come on, Bottle Rabbit, there's nothing to it.' The rabbit sighed again, 'Oh, all right then.'

'Great. Thanks much, old man. Then I'll be on my way. See you. Have a good one.' And Ken thumped off at high speed. Then he stopped and raced back, 'Mercy. I nearly forgot. Be sure to hold on to that old purse till I come back for it, and be sure and remind the Lamb not to open the Teak Box and try to use it till the end of this week. That's Tuesday next, July Third.'

'Why not? asked the rabbit.

'Why not? Because - er - because the ink'll slop out, that's why. The Lamb'll know. Just tell him that. Wait for the ink to set, tell him.'

'Oh, all right, Ken, but I'm not absolutely sure I ...'

'Fine, great, thanks a lot, see you,' gabbled Ken; and he was off into the undergrowth, his big pig-legs thumping away, thumping away.

The rabbit stood there holding the quite heavy Teak Box, a timid smile on his kind face. He hoped nothing fishy was going on. More than one forest creature on and off had called Ken a Confidence Pig in his hearing. And he half-knew they were right at least some of the time. But the Bottle Rabbit really did like this handsome and charming if rather stout animal.

Up came a Lamb.

'Excuse me, have you seen a big pig with a Teak Box?'

'Ken's just left this minute,' replied the Bottle Rabbit. The Lamb looked crestfallen and bleated delicately. 'However, he left this for you,' went on the rabbit. He showed the Lamb the Teak Box.

'Goody,' piped the woolly animal, and he skipped about, lamb-like. 'So Ken didn't forget me then. Oh,

5

how I love that kindly pig. I met him at the bus station. He told me my fortune's made, you know.' The Lamb stroked the Teak Box tenderly. 'Oh, I nearly forgot. I'm supposed to give Ken this purse full of money'.

Now the Bottle Rabbit gave a startled hop.

'Of *money*? Ken didn't say anything to me about money.' The Lamb smiled calmly.

'Oh yes, it's my savings you see. Ken's going to double it, treble it, even quaddlepull it for me.'

'Really? How?'

'Well, he has this wonderful machine; you put your money in and it comes out a lot more. He showed me. Ken put in a pound and four pounds came out. It's the same machine as this Teak Box here, except Ken's is ready already; the ink's set, or something; I've got to wait a week with mine. Then I can go on using it and using it, and having lots and lots of money.'

The Bottle Rabbit liked money quite a lot himself, as a matter of fact, so he pricked up his long floppy ears. But he felt a bit bothered; you never knew with Ken.

'Well,' bleated the Lamb, 'am I supposed to give you the purse now?' The Bottle Rabbit, still bothered, nodded, 'I suppose so, ' and the Lamb, baa-ing contentedly, handed over his purse full of savings. It was a shabby, worn leather purse, not all that heavy.

At the feel of the innocent Lamb's sad purse the Bottle Rabbit made up his mind. Though sometimes perhaps a little slow to grasp things, this simple rabbit could be very firm indeed when necessary. 'Look', he said, 'I want to help you. I've always been particularly fond of sheep - lambs, too, for that matter. This box of yours, it could be all right, but I just want to check a few things with Ken. It'll only take a couple of hours.' The Lamb looked unhappy.

6

'Can't I have my lovely Teak Box now then?' the little animal baa-ed.

'Don't worry; it won't be long. Look. Take your purse back for now. Are you hungry?'

'A bit, 'bleated the Lamb, 'I missed breakfast. I was so excited.'

'Well', said the rabbit, 'Just go into my friends' cabin here. They love animals dropping in. There's milk, Chelsea buns and some baked beans in the kitchen, and tea to drink. So have a bite to eat, read a book or take a little snooze; I'll be back soon.'

'Thank you very much,' baa-ed the Lamb. 'You will be careful with my Teak Box, though?' The rabbit promised he'd look after it very carefully.

So the Lamb ambled into the cabin, and the rabbit began to inspect the Teak Box.

'It's a Bugatti job, I know it is,' he whispered to himself. 'I bet it's another one of Ken's Bugatti tricks.' (The Bottle Rabbit was remembering a time when he'd been taken in by Ken. He'd once actually swapped his Magic Bottle for a fake Bugatti car of Ken's that didn't go. Of course he'd got his Bottle back, with help from Forest friends).

'Well, I'm going to risk it,' he said to himself, 'I'm going to have a look at this famous money-making machinery, ink or no ink.' And the rabbit boldly fiddled with the lid. The Teak Box opened easily enough. Peering inside, he saw a rusting flat-iron and a monkey wrench wrapped in oily string. Nothing else.

Pursing his lips, the rabbit closed the Teak Box, took it up in his paws and hopped off straight towards the pig's Forest home. 'Why does Ken do these things?' he asked himself. 'That poor Lamb. He's being tricked just like I was once.' He knew that this time he had to have it out with Ken.

———

More surprises were to come, though. As he neared Ken's house, a long-haired stoat stepped out from behind a willow tree and stopped him politely.

'Excuse me. You are the Bottle Rabbit, aren't you?'

'Yes, I am.' The stoat blushed faintly.

'I hope you don't mind my asking, but I wonder what you think of my *Autumn Thoughts*?'

'Sorry?' said the rabbit pricking up his long ears.

'*Autumn Thoughts*, my poem, don't you remember? It begins:

> Leaves damped,
> Hearts clamped,
> Throats dry,
> Stoats cry.
> A dying season,
> 'Tis nature's foison.

8

That's how it begins. Don't you remember? I bring pigs in later.'

The Bottle Rabbit felt puzzled. Stoats? Pigs? And hadn't Ken said something about poems just now? Was this another of his schemes? What was going on?

'What's going on?' he asked the eager but bashful stoat.

'Then you haven't read *Autumn Thoughts* yet?' said the stoat. 'It was my entry for your Bottle Rabbit Prize Poem Contest. I sent it to you last week, you see, care of Ken the Pig, Stye Hall, with 90p and a bag of marsh-mallows like it said in the advert. Perhaps the poem isn't any good? P'raps you don't like marshmallows? I could get something else.' The stoat smiled anxiously.

'What next?' said the rabbit to himself, 'I've never had a Prize Poem Contest. Ken's at it again.' He gazed at the stoat and said firmly, 'Look, all this can be worked out. Give me an hour or two. I'll tell you what; are you hungry?'

'Well, I am rather,' said the stoat, 'I missed breakfast. I was writing more poems and didn't think...'

'Well, if you'll go and wait for me at Fred and Charlie's cabin - you know - near the Beech Grove, you'll find stuff to eat, buns and baked beans and stuff. There's a friendly Lamb there who'll keep you company.'

'Oh all right, I'll go and wait there,' sighed the stoat. 'Well, toodle-oo. I think you'll like *Autumn Thoughts*'. And the stoat-poet shuffled off, waving his paws in the sky.

———

As the Bottle Rabbit hopped on toward Stye Hall he

was mentally scratching his head. What on earth was this all about, then? Why would the stoat send poems to him? Not that he didn't like poetry. When he got to Stye Hall (an attractive three-bedroomed bungalow. The pig had built his house with bricks so the wind couldn't blow it down), he saw that the front door was half open, and inside the floor was piled with bulgy parcels. And the odd thing was that they were all addressed to *him*: Bottle Rabbit Poem Prize, they said, c/o Ken the Pig, Chief Judge, Stye Hall. There was also a yellow note from the Post Office saying there were more parcels waiting to be picked up.

The rabbit clambered over heaps of parcels and went on into the hall. As he put down the Teak Box on Ken's hat-stand a leaflet caught his eye. It said:

Grand Poetry Compatition!!!

SPONSARD BY THE BOTTLE RABBIT
BIG BIG PRIZES

All Winning Entries will be Printed.
PIG THEMES encouraged.

Send your poem (not too long) to:
Bottle Rabbit
c/o Ken the Pig, Stye Hall, The Forest

Rules: Inclose your name and address
and *Plenty of Presents and money*. Chief
Judge of Poems, Ken the Pig, B.A.

The Bottle Rabbit whistled and shook his head in wonder. He thought for a minute. 'Well,' he said to himself. 'All these parcels are addressed to me. I think

I'm going to open some.' And he started pulling at tape and string and brown paper. Each parcel had a poem in it, and a present, and sometimes some coins, too. The poems seemed mostly to be in praise of pigs. One began:

Oh wild west pig thou breath of autumn's being...

Another:
The awful shadow of some unseen Pig
Floats though unseen amongst us...

A third:
Pig!
Why soarest thou above that tomb?'
To what sublime and starry-paven home
Floatest thou?

The presents were boxes of chocolates, bags of sweets, baskets of fruit, packets of nuts, tins of baked beans, and cardboard boxes containing various bottles, including three each of pickled onions and of Australian brandy. The rabbit went on dazedly opening parcel after parcel. One had no present in it at all, just a nasty sort of poem beginning:
'An old, mad, blind, despised and dying pig...' with a note at the bottom: 'Ha ha. You can't catch me that way. Signed: Max Ramm, Rockcliffe Road, the Town.'
Just as he'd finished reading this nasty poem and note, the rabbit heard a happy grunting and whistling, and up came Ken, pushing a wooden wheelbarrow overflowing with yet more parcels. The big pig skipped about and started to sing.
'Tirra lirra by the river,' sang Ken. But when he saw the Bottle Rabbit standing amongst the parcels his face

11

went a deep dark red. Then his whole head seemed to be blushing: cheeks, neck, nose, ears, eyelids, back of neck, everything.

'What's going on Ken?' said the rabbit.

For a moment the pig seemed at a loss for words. But he recovered fast.

'Found the parcels did you old man? Good show. We did pretty well, didn't we, in the circs?'

'We?'

'Yes, old man. You and me. Matter of fact I was just going to sort things out and send you your share.'

'Share?'

'Oh come on BR. You surely didn't think I'd keep all the spoils to myself did you? That wouldn't be cricket.'

'Spoils?'

'Yes; I think you're certainly entitled to about half of these gifts. Let's say a quarter; certainly some of them anyhow. Here's one for starters.' Ken made to hand the

12

rabbit a tin of arrowroot biscuits with a picture of a fluffy kitten on it.

The Bottle Rabbit raised a dismissive paw. 'Ken, I don't even like arrowroot biscuits anymore. I've gone off them. But anyhow that's not the point. What about the compatition - competition, I mean - all those trusting animals who've sent you poems and presents?' Ken smiled.

'No problem old man. No winners, that's all. General standard too low this year. Nothing came up to scratch. We'll keep the lot.' Ken laughed heartily, but then saw the horrified look on the rabbit's kind face and tried again.

'Well, I suppose at a pinch we could pull a couple of them out of a hat, type 'em up and send 'em over to *The Forest Echo*, or better still *The Advertiser* ... they'll print anything and glad to.' Ken began rooting amongst the parcels again and came up smilingly holding out a round, powdery, sugary box. 'Here, try this Turkish Delight, old man. It's first rate. The chap's poem's too long though; he's calling it 'The Triumph of Life'. I like his title but the poem's much too long.' As he chattered on Ken was munching away and rooting and delving among the parcels, every now and then pocketing clinking coins and rustling bank-notes.

The Bottle Rabbit took a deep breath.

'Ken, this is just a racket isn't it? What they call a Confidence Trick? You're going to keep all the presents and money, and not give away any big prizes at all. And why did you put my name down as Sponsor, Ken, without asking; that's not fair you know.'

Ken began plunging about and trying to laugh heartily again, all the time glancing at the Bottle Rabbit with his shrewd little eyes.

'Not a *racket* old man, that's not a very nice word.

More an Encouragement Programme for Writing Animals. And why you as sponsor you ask? It's obvious old man. Every animal in the Forest knows you're a kind, decent-hearted rabbit. Not the brightest perhaps, no... excuse me BR... slip of the tongue... one of the brightest, one of the best, one we can all trust. That sort of thing old man. And it's worked like a charm. One of my smartest ploys. The poems have come pouring in. *And* the presents... we're sitting pretty...' Ken glanced at the rabbit, still didn't like the look on his face and trailed off, trying to change the subject. 'Didn't see that confounded beaver looking for me, did you, anywhere, old man?'

'Ken.' The Bottle Rabbit was doing his best to look stern, 'Ken, it's not fair.'

The pig took off his alpine hat and stroked its chamois brush.

'All's fair in love and war, old man. You know that.' He dug the rabbit in the ribs, smiling anxiously.

'Ken, I'm sorry, it's not right.'

'Oh come on old man. No harm done. All in a spirit of fair play and love of books.'

'Ken - really - I'm not that much of a dumbo you know'.

But even as he spoke the Bottle Rabbit couldn't help grinning a bit at Ken's way of putting things, and at the handsome dare-devil lifting of Ken's nose, and at his witty, elegant trotter-movements. Soon he was laughing hard and then they were both laughing hard.

'It's no good, though, Ken,' spluttered the Bottle Rabbit as he wiped his eyes, 'All these poems and presents have to go back - all of them.' The big pig, encouraged by the laughter, was bracing himself for one last protest when a sudden huge shadow loomed over the doorway.

'Don't tell me; I know it, I know it, I know it,' groaned Ken.

———

'All well here I trust?' boomed a deep voice. 'Ah, my dear Bottle Rabbit. How pleasant to see you. And hullo there, Ken. Hullo there. What a delightful home you have here. And what a lot of post you're getting these days. Yes. I heard about your poetry prizes; some very keen poetry-writing stoats spoke of it to me. I hope it all goes swimmingly and may the best animal win.'

'Right, Sam, as always you are absolutely right.' Ken ground this out through his teeth. But Sam the Bear (for that of course was who it was) raised a huge paw. He had not finished speaking.

'Or better still, Ken - much better still - you will decide to send back all poems and all presents. Yes. Much better that, for the general good of the forest and of your good self. Bottle Rabbit, I am sure you will be ready to give us a full account of Ken's clearing-up work over tea this evening at Fred and Charlie's.' Sam beamed round, patted Ken heavily on the back, and padded off.

'I don't believe it. I just don't believe it, 'cried Ken loudly. The pig plucked off his alpine hat and dashed it to the ground. 'It's always the same, always. Sam's forever pushing that huge nose of his into my business. I don't like it old man, I really don't.' The Bottle Rabbit smiled,

'Come on Ken. You know Sam's right. Of course you've got to send the stuff back. Come on, I'll give you a hand with the packing and posting.'

15

And that's what they did. Ken picked up his hat again and went to work, grumbling.

'It's all very well for Sam, but this is costing me a fortune in stamps alone,' he kept muttering.

Yet soon he cheered up. In fact all afternoon the pig managed to eat plenty of Turkish Delight, marsh mallows and other dainties that he found in the parcels,

and the Bottle Rabbit was never absolutely sure that all the coins and notes the poets had sent got back into their envelopes. Interested in money as he was, he understood Ken's excitement very well.

Ken clearly enjoyed reading the pig-praise poems, too. 'Listen to this one,' he'd grunt, then stop work and read it out loud, sometimes two or three times. It slowed things down. There was so much stuff to take back to the Post Office that in the end they had to get a badger. It was that morning's badger with his wheelbarrow.

'Had your little kip then? Cheers,' he said to Ken. The big pig looked dignified and did not reply.

As they were leaving with the last load, Ken took one more look at the Turkish Delight poem. 'Hey, wait a minute, listen to this,' he cried.

> Swift as a spirit hastening to his task
> Of glory and of good, the Pig sprang forth
> Rejoicing in his splendour, and the mask
> Of darkness fell from the awakening Earth.

Ken plumped about smilingly.

'BR, I like it, I like it. Let's give it a prize, some marshmallows or something.'

But the Bottle Rabbit had stopped listening. He'd just remembered the Lamb, and why he'd come to see the pig. Now he was pointing at the Teak Box on Ken's hat-stand in a meaningful way.

'Well, Ken?'

The pig goggled at the Teak Box.

'Where on earth did you get hold of that, old man?' The Bottle Rabbit shook his head,

'You gave it to me this very morning, Ken.'

'Oh, yes, of course. Er, you didn't open it did you, old man?'

'Yes, Ken. And I also had a chat with the Lamb. He thought it was a money-machine, but I've seen the monkey-wrench, the rusty flat-iron and the oily string.'

Ken went off into another of his hollow guffaws.

'Isn't it awfully good? The monkey-wrench? The

string? One of my best leg-pulls... The Lamb will be frightfully amused. He knows my fun. Er.. you did bring along that shabby old purse of his? I said I'd take it off the little creature's hands.'

'No, I didn't, Ken,' said the Bottle Rabbit quite warmly, thinking of that harmless animal's savings. For a moment he was really fed up with Ken. 'I gave the Lamb back his purse.' The pig's big face fell.

'You shouldn't have done that, old man, you really shouldn't. It might have come in handy for a rainy day.'

Now it was the Bottle Rabbit's turn to be lost for words. Then he said loudly and firmly:

'KEN! YOU ARE IMPOSSIBLE!' The pig smirked.

'Oh I wouldn't say that old man. Definitely not. I tell you what, though, it's getting towards tea-time. Why don't you set to and pongle us up some buns and a nice cup of chah?'

'Oh, well, what's the use? I give up,' said the Bottle Rabbit to himself. 'Ken's Ken and there it is. At least I've saved the Lamb's money for him.' He raised his Bottle and did a two-pongler: 'Pongle... Pongle.' A good brown pot of tea quickly arrived, with cucumber sandwiches, tea-cakes and six Bakewell tarts. As rabbit and pig sat munching and gulping, Ken told many a saucy pig-joke; afterwards, with his mouth still full of Bakewell tart, he sang some of his happy pig-songs. He was wearing high-heeled boots, and clacked up and down from time to time. The truth is the Bottle Rabbit really loved being with Ken when he was like this.

But, 'Goodness,' the rabbit suddenly exclaimed, 'I must go. It's getting late. There's those two animals at Fred and Charlie's, that Lamb and that stoat-poet; what will they be thinking? Come on, Ken, it's time for tea.' Ken stared at him.

'You mean me at Fred and Charlie's? With Sam?

'Well... yes.' Ken shook his head wonderingly.

'BR, are you mad? I mean, pull yourself together old man.' The rabbit stared back at him, puzzled. Ken shook his head again.

'Well, never mind old man, let's leave it at that; I'll explain another day.' He glanced at his plump wrist-watch, 'Time's up, BR. See you in the fullness.' And with extraordinary speed and delicacy the big pig twinkled off, disappearing into the woods, singing away.

The Bottle Rabbit loyally shook his head, 'I'll never make him out, but good old Ken, after all, 'he thought, 'he knows best what to do. After all there's no one quite like Ken.'

———————

It was nearly six o'clock when the rabbit burst in through Fred and Charlie's door. 'Sorry everybody. Sorry I'm late. I was with...' But then he saw that everybody was quietly drinking tea. Sam sat in one corner holding up wool for that startlingly beautiful white cat, Emily. She was knitting a dark green jumper (for me? the Bottle Rabbit wondered). Sam's wife Maud was reading *The Advertiser*. The Lamb was cheerfully helping Fred to bake some scones, and the stoat-poet was reading aloud from one of Charlie's big books of poetry: Charlie, a great poetry-lover, sat smoking his curvy pipe with his eyes closed, one hoof waving in time to the poem's rhythm.

'Now here's one of my own. It's called *Autumn Thoughts*, the stoat was saying. Charlie's hoof went on waving. Animals nodded and smiled at the Bottle

19

Rabbit, but nobody asked any awkward questions. So he kept quiet.

Over a fish supper that night, the Bottle Rabbit had a little chat with the Lamb, who seemed to have forgotten all about his Teak Box hopes.

And Wednesday ended quietly, with early bed all round. As the rabbit began falling asleep, with the Lamb snore-bleating beside him and Emily not far away, he pondered over the day's goings-on. Ken the Pig and his Teak Box and his Poetry Prizes first came up, but thinking about Ken at bed-time? No, Ken was just too puzzling for this time of night. So he thought about his lovely Magic Bottle instead, and a sleepy thought swam up. He'd often pongled once and pongled twice, for drinks and sandwiches, and often enough he'd pongled four times or five times, for Mice or for Blue Hares; he couldn't remember about six, but he'd certainly done seven for the Golden Eagle and General Alarum, and once eight times for a Feast. The rabbit now gave a slow, huge yawn, and thought, sleepily, why is it somehow I've never done a three-pongler? What happens with that, I wonder? Perhaps I'll do a three-pongle this week. Perhaps next Sunday with Emily. I bet three'll be a bit strange; threes always are. He snuggled down sleepily among the bleating lamb-snores.

Somehow the young Lamb and all these sleepy numbers had shifted his mind towards his friend, the little counting rabbit, Count Hubert. 'I sometimes wonder whether Hubert could even count as far as three without something going wrong most times,' he mused. Yawn-smiling at this thought the Bottle Rabbit drifted off into restful sleep, joining all the other animals in Fred and Charlie's cabin.

Count Hubert Gets On His Bike

'Ahem! Ahem! 1...3...4...2,' Count Hubert counted quietly and quickly, in soft spurts, to himself. He loved counting, though he usually got it all wrong. The little rabbit was perched on the saddle of a brand-new bicycle.

Now he spoke out loud: 'Ahem! Ahem! 1...3...2...I'm off!' And he stamped down hard on a pedal with his right back-paw. In about ten seconds he *was* off, head over heels in a hawthorn hedge, with his bicycle deep in a black-currant bush, its handlebars twisted, its front wheel still twirling and twirling. Count Hubert had forgotten all about balancing and all about steering.

It was a proper grown-up kind of bicycle, mind you - no childish fat tyres, no wide, podgy saddle, just a plain dark blue bike, with a 3-speed, a large bell on the handlebars and a real leather saddlebag. The little rabbit had been so excited and happy that he'd missed breakfast. But he'd put a picnic lunch in his bag; lettuce and tomato sandwiches with wholemeal bread, and a bottle of fizzy lemonade: also a comic-book called *The Count of Monte Cristo* to read if he got tired.

His Uncle Emsworth had given him the bicycle for his birthday, a great kindness, as his Uncle only had his pension.

'This should keep you busy, my boy,' the grey-haired old rabbit had said.

'Oh yes Uncle, it's lovely.'

'I expect you'll be wanting to go off on plenty of long, healthy rides, off in other directions, I mean.'

'Oh yes, I shall, Uncle Emsworth, and then I'll come back and tell you all about it, my rides and my bike and what I've counted and everything.' 'Oh, I shouldn't bother about doing that, dear boy,' his Uncle said, as he patted Hubert on the head. 'Just get in plenty of long, enjoyable rides. Good long rides.'

So here he was, this excitable young cousin of the Bottle Rabbit, stuck in a hedge heaped with May. But, smiling and shaking his head and rubbing his elbow, the little animal had soon scrambled up out of it, his small brown shoulders all flecked with snowy petals. The bicycle wasn't really damaged, just a bit scratched, and the handlebars twisted, but to cheer himself up thoroughly before starting off again he began some breathless counting: 'Ahem! Ahem! 1... 4... 2... 47... 19... 6... 193...'

A strong voice interrupted him:

'What's all this, then? Riding to the endangerment of the public are we? On the public thoroughfare? And why aren't you at school?' A heavy bulldog in police-sergeant's uniform, not looking at all friendly, was eyeing his bent machine. Count Hubert swallowed.

'I'm just counting the spokes on my new bike, sir, at the moment. Just spoke-counting. But mostly I'm learning to ride it. It's Thursday. It's our half-holiday, sir.'

The sergeant stood there, one gloved paw steadying his own tall bicycle, with its fat black handle-grips heating in the sunlight.

'That's all very well,' he grunted; his big jowl wobbled. 'But there's other animals to take into account. My advice to you, my lad, is to keep off the

public thoroughfare till you know what you're doing.'

'I'll definitely do my very best sir.' The bulldog nodded.

'Now straighten those twisted handlebars.' The rabbit, with nervous paws, did this as best as he could.

'Right then. I'll be keeping an eye on you, my lad.' And, big jowl still wobbling, the bulldog climbed back on to his high black bike. His boot pushed off and the bicycle ticked, ticked, ticked.

———

Watching him go with downcast eyes, Count Hubert sighed a little sigh. But as mostly he was a happy animal, full of bounce and cheerfulness, he soon began practising again, zigging and zagging along the country lanes, gradually straightening out and straightening out until he could go quite long distances without any stops and starts at all. It suddenly became a lovely feeling, just whizzing along and whizzing along, the tyres thrumming, the spokes twinkling and clinking. All the air was light; fresh green trees flashed by. His quick eyes blinked happily, his tender lips quivered. And he burst into a favourite song:

> The King was in his counting-house
> Counting out his money,
> The Queen was in her parlour
> Eating bread and hon...

Nothing lasts. THUMP. BUMP. SCRUDGE. And there little Hubert was, down in the dust again. Not altogether down, though. The rabbit had a feeling that he'd just done some rather skilful dodging. What's more, when he started up from the ditch he had landed in his eyes met the beady eyes of an old acquaintance. It was the Golden Baker.

'Phew,' said the Golden Baker, 'that was a close shave. I thought you were out for the count that time.'

Count Hubert struggled up dustily, rubbing his ankle as the Baker went on talking.

'Got a bike now, have you? Better watch yourself on the public thoroughfare, lad. Animals come rushing round corners you know. Then... Bang!... I've seen it happen on countless occasions, countless...' Count Hubert started to speak, but the Golden Baker ploughed on:

'You've got to keep an eye out, Hubert. Watch out for the other fellow. That's what I always say, watch out for the other fellow. You can't be too careful.' He spun the pedals of his tricycle and wiped his lips. 'We can count ourselves lucky nothing worse happened.'

Count Hubert felt a bit put out. After all it was the Baker who had just trundled round the corner quite fast in the very middle of the road on his large tricycle, not doing any watching out for the other fellow at all. But he shrugged and smiled and picked up his dark blue bicycle again. There was nothing much wrong: a bruised ankle, twisted handlebars, and on his bike another scratch or two.

'Ahem! Ahem! or 4... or 21... or 11... or 8... or 5...' The little rabbit was off again, counting away at the scratches, lips moving fast, ears twitching like anything.

'Nice little bit of dodging you did, mind you, 'interrupted the Golden Baker, straightening the rabbit's twisted handlebars as he spoke, 'I thought we were in for a Bang, myself. You did very well, I will say that. Here. Have one of my best pies. Fresh-baked. Here, take it. I'll let you have it at a discount. No, I'm only joking, it's a present.'

And with that the Baker reached down into his fragrant sort of cupboard-on-wheels and pulled out a fine hot steaming golden-crusted pork pie.

Count Hubert blushed.

'Thank you very much, Golden Baker. It's really kind; especially as I nearly bashed into you, banged into you I mean. But all I ever eat is vegetables and cheese.'

'Well. No accounting for tastes,' said the Baker, 'Cheers.' And he took a big bite out of the pie himself, rolled his eyes in pleasure, then gulped down the rest of it. 'That was a beauty, though I say it myself,' he gasped, wiping his lips. 'One of my triumphs. Cheers, then. I've got to be off. Take care.'

As the Golden Baker tricycled off in one direction, Count Hubert bicycled slowly off in the other. Somehow everything had gone a bit grey. What with the police bulldog and now this near-accident, bicycling was turning out more complicated than he'd thought.

But pleasanter times were in store. Wobbling up a pebbly road and into an ash grove he came upon a stately country house. Three beagles eyed him through three of its large ground floor windows. 'Ahem! Ahem! 1...5...4...173...19...6,' the little rabbit was at it yet again; now he was counting the window panes. He'd done a whole side when the front door opened and a smiling animal he knew quite well filled the door space. it was Maud the Bear, Sam's ample, comfortable wife. Maud was a skilful golfer, not bad at tennis, and she worked as a part-time cook, famous for her meringues.

'Well, bless me, 'cried Maud in her deep voice, 'if it isn't the little counter himself. And what brings you out here so far from home?'

'Practising my bike.'

'And what a lovely bike it is. I love dark blue as a colour. Collected a few scratches I see. And aren't your handlebars twisted, dear?'

'I expect so,' said Count Hubert, sighing, as he lent his bicycle against a fence, not far from somebody else's bicycle.

The three handsome beagles he'd seen in the window now came springing out of the house, baying, Maud introduced them:

'Count Hubert, this is Bard, this is Burt, and this is Berm'

'Well, you'd better come in, as you're here, barked

Bard, and all animals moved inside and sat down.

Conversation became general.

'Why did Maud call you the counter, just now?' asked Burt in a friendly way. 'Oh. I count, you know,' said the little rabbit.

'Well,' growled Bard, 'we all count, don't we? Somewhere, in the general scheme of things?'

'No, no. I mean I count numbers. I'm good at it, you see.'

'Oh. That kind of counting. But, then, can't we all...'

'And how are the poodles today?' broke in Maud, tactfully changing the subject.

'Off doing their Thursday shopping,' said Berm.

'It's Japanese stuff today, 'said Burt.

'They're obsessed,' said Bard, 'weird tastes they have, those four. But now,' turning to Count Hubert, 'I suppose you're counting on getting a bit to eat? We like animals just dropping in don't we, Berm?' Bard certainly sounded gruff, but Berm and Burt laughed.

'Don't mind Bard,' said Burt, 'His bark is worse than his bite. Just make yourself comfortable.' And Bard, Burt and Berm loped off into the kitchen. Soon beagle-barking and beagle-laughing could be heard out there.

'Does all this whole house belong to the beagles, then?' Count Hubert asked Maud, as they sat about.

'No, no. They just live and work here. It all belongs to four wealthy poodles. Very rich dogs. With very loud voices.'

'What do the poodles do?'

'They mostly just lounge. They're well looked after, of course. Good books, good music, good food. Lovely garden. it's not a bad life all round.'

Lunch was a success.

'It's only carrot soup with coriander, and cheese

sandwiches today,' said Burt. 'We have to count the calories you know.'

How on earth do you count *them*? Count Hubert wondered to himself, as he spooned up his delicious soup. Afterwards there was one of Maud's big meringues. Then Berm sang a lovely lute-song for counter-tenor, Burt told an extremely funny joke, Bard did a clever trick with an egg and a spoon, and Maud countered with some of her imitations.

This party was interrupted when loud yappings announced the poodles' return. Four slim and elegant figures flashed upstairs, laden with packages. 'They've got an accountant fellow doing things up there today,' said Berm, 'counting their money, I dare say.' He stood up. 'Well, back to work.' And he and Burt moved into the kitchen to join Maud.

'Count me out,' said Bard. 'It's my afternoon off.'

'I think I'd better be off, then,' said Count Hubert.

'Yes. Goodbye,' barked Bard. 'Come again sometime; we'll let you know' The beagle settled down on the sofa with a cigar.

———————

What friendly and cheerful animals, thought Count Hubert to himself, pedalling on, even though Bard had seemed on the gruff side. Probably only his fun, he thought. His bicycle was feeling heavier than before, but he put this down to lunch.

He rode on smoothly now, heading towards home and humming a cheerful hymn tune, 'Count Your Blessings Every Day.' He was amusedly ringing his bell, keeping time, when out of a gorse bush leapt a muscular ferret in gleaming spectacles.

'Stop thief!' the ferret snarled. 'Stop now, or prepare to take the consequences.' And a scrawny but powerful wrist shot out to grab the little rabbit's handlebars. Down went Hubert yet again, bumping his elbows. Also a handlebar caught him on the side of the head, quite hard.

He scrambled up, rubbing his head.

'What on earth did you do that for?' he cried.

'Bold as brass, isn't he?' the ferret asked, his sharp snout peering round everywhere, though there was no one there to answer. 'Calmly steals a bike, then calmly complains?' The ferret's name was Baxter, and he was panting a bit, out of breath from running.

'I haven't stolen any bikes. This is *my* bike. It's dark blue. It's got a 3-speed. My Uncle Emsworth gave it me for my birthday.'

'Just listen to him. So now it's his Uncle. And birthdays. A likely tale.' The ferret panted some more. 'I'll tell you what. You can say all that to the sergeant. The

29

police station's just down the road past those oak trees. Come on. And no nonsense or else.' Baxter's thick spectacles gleamed. He grabbed the little Count's shoulder in one sharp-clawed paw, and with another paw clutching the bicycle's twisted handlebars he marched the rabbit all the way to a brick building that said POLICE in big letters over the door.

'He's going to have to account for himself now. He's in for it now.' The ferret did horrible skips of pleasure. 'He's in for it now,'he muttered again and again. Count Hubert was dumbfounded at this turn of events.

In no time at all he was in the police station being growled at by a sergeant sitting in his shirt-sleeves behind a mahogany counter, bootlaces undone. The sergeant's jowl wobbled; it was that same heavy bulldog, and his helmet lay on the counter.

'So it's you again, young fellow-me-lad. Never out of trouble. You can take your paw off him, ferret. What is it this time, then?'

'Nothing. I was just riding my bike, when...'

'His bike! His bike!' Baxter screeched. 'That's my sister Agatha's new bike, as well he knows. I borrowed Aggie's bike this morning to go to the poodles. My car's gone wonky again; I think it's the choke. She's an accountant my sister, same as I am. You can see it's Aggie's bike. It's got a different sort of cross-bar arrangement. It hasn't *got* a cross-bar.' The bulldog looked slowly from ferret to rabbit.

'What's a cross-bar?' asked Count Hubert meekly.

'It doesn't matter,' snapped Baxter. 'We want our bike back, and we want this burglar in prison.'

The bulldog reached for a long black book, licked a paw, and leafed through it until he found a fresh page. Count Hubert was frightened now, and stood there with his head down and his back bent.

'This'll all have to be written up,' grunted the bulldog. 'Take any phone calls Trevor, I'm going to be busy', he barked over his shoulder to another bulldog in the back room, 'Right, Howard,' Trevor barked back, gruffly.

'Been in trouble already today, haven't you, rabbit, with bicycles?' The sergeant stared him up and down and the little rabbit blinked back at him unhappily. 'This one's looking serious. Sounds like a County Court Case to me. Name?'

'Oh. Er. It's Count Hubert.' The big bulldog leaned over his counter and eyed the poor little animal sternly.

'So what have you got to say for yourself - Hubert, is it? - before I lock you up?'

'Lock me up?' The rabbit shivered. Then he thought of something. 'Look! I can prove it's my bike,' he cried.

'Oh yes? How're you doing that, then?'

'If you'll just open that saddlebag you'll see what's inside. But first I can tell you what's inside - lettuce and tomato sandwiches from home, some lemonade, the fizzy kind, and a book with my name in it; it's called *The Count of Monte Cristo*. That'll prove the bike's mine, won't it?'

'Right then. Let's have a look,' grunted the bulldog. 'We'll give you the benefit of the doubt, for the time being. But I'll tell you now, I don't like it.' Baxter suddenly coughed loudly. The ferret was looking very red in the face.

'Ah. No need to bother yourself about that saddlebag, officer. Everything's quite in order there' but he was too late. Howard the bulldog had already unbuckled the stiff, new straps and was pulling open the flap.

All peered in. It smelt of new leather. Nothing happened for a while, until the sergeant, who had been rooting about in the bag, gave a deep bark and growled at both animals.

'What's all this then?' said the Bulldog. Things looked bad for Count Hubert. In the saddlebag were, a packet of sandwiches, yes. But not lettuce and tomato with wholemeal bread. It was spam and pickled beetroot with white sliced. No book; only a little mop. No fizzy lemonade; instead five full bottles of Scotch whisky.

The ferret had now flushed a deep, deep red.

'It's my bike, officer, my sister's, that is. It's my sandwiches. For my tea. I've always liked spam. The mop's my sister's, and the whisky... er... the whisky's a present for these poodles I do accounting for. I've just been doing them upstairs in the ash grove you know. I'm very good at accounts. Very efficient.' Baxter's spectacles gleamed. 'That's right,' he repeated, 'The poodles.. that's who the whisky's for.' Then he wheeled on Count Hubert. 'You stole all these things with my bike. You know you did. See it in your face. See it in your eye. Lazy, idle little schemer.'

Here Count Hubert spoke up bravely for himself.

'I'm not lazy, and I'm not idle. I do a lot of counting, for one thing. And I'm not a screamer, either, whatever that is.' But now Howard the bulldog was examining the bag's contents, piece by piece, and shaking his head. He looked first at Baxter.

'Accountant are you, sir? If this is your bicycle, sir, or your sister's, I can't say I think it's very clever, riding a bicycle with a saddlebag full of whisky bottles. Could have caused a nasty accident, sir, on the public thoroughfare; very unwise, sir.' The ferret's snouty face

grew redder than ever, crimson, almost.

'However,' the sergeant stared grimly at Count Hubert, 'you're the one that's in deep trouble, my lad. I'll have to take all these purloined articles into account, writing up my report.' He placed them all on the counter.

'Now. Paws out. We'll try these on for size.' And he actually slipped a pair of handcuffs over the white-faced little rabbit's trembling, delicate front paws.

'Stand there for now.' And the bulldog began pencilling it down in his black book. His thick lips formed the words 'bicycle,' 'spam,' 'mop,' 'whisky,' as he worked away.

Count Hubert stared round miserably. What on earth was happening to him? Would they lock him up? Would he be there all night? In that cell over there? With all those bars? Hopelessly, very, very slowly, he began to count the bars '1...2...3...4...5...6...7..' The sergeant, breathing heavily, went on writing. Baxter stood smirking to one side; his spectacles gleamed. The little rabbit had got to '33' and paused. Time seemed to have come to a stop.

———

Suddenly they all heard a crash, a thud and a rude word outside, and to everyone's astonishment, in staggered the beagle, Bard, breathing hard and rubbing his knee.

'There you are, Hubert. Thank goodness. I've brought you your bike. Berm found it, Burt straightened the twisted handlebars, and they made me ride it here. It's my afternoon off, you know. I always thought you had to pedal counter-clockwise on the confounded things. Then I got it right. but I kept forgetting.

Bard rubbed his knee again, and looked more closely at Count Hubert.

'But what on earth's going on here? What are they doing to you?'

'They've, they've...' But big tears now began rolling down the poor little rabbit's cheeks, and he couldn't go on.

'Stole a bike, he did,' barked the sergeant doggedly. 'And some spam and a mop and a lot of whisky.'

'Don't be absurd,' snapped Bard, 'It's all some silly mistake. There were two dark blue bikes. I've got his outside. It's got a cross-bar. It's a bit scratched, and the handlebars are twisted again.. I fell off it four times, on the public thoroughfare, I barked my shins. But it'll go all right. Count Hubert unaccountably took the wrong one after lunch. Too much lemonade I expect. Could happen to anyone. However,' Bard stared angrily through his thick glasses, 'the idea of hounding a small animal and handcuffing him for such a trivial offence. It's not as if he's a murderer or a counterfeiter. Take those irons off at once, sergeant, or I'll send a full account of all this to County Headquarters tonight.'

'He's a constant trouble-maker, you know, this Count Hubert,' grunted the bulldog, looking bothered.

'Stuff and nonsense!' He's a friend of ours. Off with the manacles and quick about it.' The Sergeant (now *he* was red in the face) lumbered over, and had just freed the little rabbit. - 'Thank you very much, Bard'. - When the keen beagle exclaimed, 'Wait a minute. What's all this fancy whisky? Wait a minute. It's malt whisky. It's the exact same brand our poodles drink. Wait a minute.' Bard picked up a bottle of the golden liquid and examined a white label on it. 'Property of Poodle Hall, Ash Grove,' he read. 'Wait a minute.' Bard looked round for Baxter.

The lithe ferret was streaking to the door.

'Stop thief!' called Bard.

Baxter didn't get far, for filling the station entrance was none other than Sam the Bear, Maud's husband, huge and black and strong.

'Stop him, Sam,' barked Bard, and the great bear simply put out a long paw and gathered the squealing ferret to his sooty bosom.

Sam had just come in to the constabulary with a blue paper about a license, but as usual he immediately took charge. Sam was a Magistrate. So. Explanations all round. Exchange of bikes. Recovery of poodles' whisky. Severe words from Sam for Baxter. Comforting words for Count Hubert. Cool words to the sergeant. Stilted words from the sergeant. Angry silence from Baxter.

Bard said he was pretty sure the poodles wouldn't lay any charges against the ferret. - 'I think he's learnt his lesson' - but did add, 'I think they'll have Agatha to do the accounts from now on. She's just as efficient as you, Baxter, and there's something about those gleaming thick specs of yours on your ferrety countenance that - Oh, well, enough said.' Bard adjusted his own thick glasses after this rather cruel speech and went on, 'Well, well, all's well that ends well, as that other Bard has it. I suggest we all go back to the ash grove (not you Baxter and not you, sergeant; you must be about your duties), and all take a little drink to calm ourselves down. Well, well. Visitors again. Berm and Burt will be overjoyed. *I'm* overjoyed.'

Baxter glared at everyone, streaked out of the station and sped off on his sister's bike. Meanwhile, Bard had packed the whisky bottles in plastic bags. 'Ahem! Ahem! 1... 5... 2... 19... 46... 8...' Count Hubert was counting, or rather, miscounting, happily again.

It was time to go. Sam nodded severely to the sergeant. Howard's jowl wobbled. Trevor, the other bulldog, watching from a station window, shook his head and twisted his handlebar moustache as bear and beagle strode off through the woods. Count Hubert was keeping up with them, on his bike, in a wobbly way.

'Don't worry, Hubert,' said Sam, 'We'll soon see your bike to rights, straighten those twisted handlebars for you'.

'Thank goodness I'm free', bubbled Hubert, 'and not in prison, and I've got my bike back, and my lunch, and I can't wait to tell Uncle Emsworth all about it, I mean recount the whole thing to him. He'll like that.' Sam patted him on the head.

PONGLE!

As they neared the Ash Grove, Burt and Berm and Maud were all standing at the door. Drinks and meringues were already set out on a table. Somewhere upstairs the four poodles were calling back and forth.

———

Later that evening, Sam took Count Hubert and his bike back to Fred and Charlie's cabin. Emily and the Bottle Rabbit were also there, drinking tea with the badger girls, and all received Count Hubert especially kindly. Sam soon started to tell the bicycle story at length:

'I had a brief encounter with Howard at the station this afternoon,' he began. While he was talking, Charlie quietly passed a bag of hundreds-and-thousands to the delighted little rabbit, who loved munching them by the pawful. Sam talked on; animals got sleepy, espe-

cially Count Hubert. When he'd finished his sweets and had some cocoa, he began to nod his head in sleepiness. Sam was still talking and talking. 'I gave this ferret Baxter a good dressing down'. So Emily and the Bottle Rabbit together quietly carried the little rabbit upstairs and tucked him into bed. He went straight to sleep, and they tiptoed away, leaving him breathing in soft spurts, his long, lean little paws lying out on the counterpane.

Plunging in the Water-Meadow

'Of course young Hubert had made a mistake with the bikes,' mused Fred, out loud, as he dried the breakfast dishes. 'And that rather nasty ferret, Baxter, was right, in a way.' The great Clydesdale was watching out of the kitchen window as Count Hubert wobbled past, off to school on his new bicycle.

'Yes, and I suppose you could say the same of Howard. I mean he really did think Hubert was a thief,' murmured Emily, as she stretched on the window sill in the bright late-June morning sun.

The Bottle Rabbit was still munching toast and gulping milk. He looked from one to the other, puzzled.

'But surely Baxter should never have pushed him off his bike like that,' he protested, his mouth full of toast. 'Even if he did think he'd stolen it. And Baxter really did try to steal the poodles' whisky. He was worse than Ken on Wednesday, really. And that bulldog didn't need to put handcuffs on poor little Hubert. I mean he'd never steal anything would he? Any more than Ken the Pig would, really'.

He was blushing a bit, making such a long speech. In the back-ground Charlie seemed to be both nodding and shaking his great carthorse head. Nothing much more was said for the time being.

Later that day Emily and the Bottle Rabbit set out, paw in paw, to buy the groceries; they always did on Fridays. As they wandered through the woodland's light and shade Emily made a quiet suggestion.

'Let's drop in and have a chat first with the badger-girls. They're by themselves this weekend, looking after their aunt's cottage; they might like visitors.'

'Good idea. It's this way isn't it?' And the Bottle Rabbit hopped over a stile into a water-meadow gleaming with the greenest grass, dotted with daisies and celandine.

'It's lovely here, let's do some plunging,' he called to Emily. 'Come on let's.' Emily smiled.

'Well, why not, after all?'

And she put down her shopping basket under a hazel-nut tree. Soon both animals were plunging and jumping and rolling and skipping and plunging through the meadow. It was one of their best games together. The field was bursting with blossom, so when

they got tired they lay down for a bit among the meadow-sweet and willow-herb and then started finding and naming flowers. It was another of their games.

'Bluebells and Borage,' said the Bottle Rabbit.

'Crane's-bill and Coltsfoot,' said Emily.

'Pennywort and Pansies.'

'Forget-me-nots and Fleabane.'

'Yellow Irises and Yellow Cress.'

'Purple Loosestrife and Purple Loosestrife!'

'What!' said the Bottle Rabbit. 'It counts twice, there's so much of it,' said Emily, laughing. Then she stopped laughing and said, in a plain, even voice,

'Deadly Nightshade.'

'Where?'

'Over by those dry stones.' Both animals shivered.

'It's a bit damp in this water-meadow' said the Bottle Rabbit. 'Yes,' said Emily, picking up her basket. 'Time to be moving on. Is your Magic Bottle in place? After all that plunging?' His paw shot up to his Bottle-pocket. All was well.

'Thanks for reminding me.'

Back to the dark woods they went and wandered down a path full of light and shade that led to a charming woodland cottage. 'Sett House,' it said on a polished piece of beechwood outside. An old hand-cart stood up-ended outside a front door wreathed in honeysuckle and climbing roses.

They knocked. No answer. They knocked again. Again no answer. They looked at one another. 'You know how late badgers sleep, Emily,' said the rabbit. 'All day, sometimes. They stay up so late at night, they often miss breakfast.'

'The door's ajar,' said Emily.

41

'A jar?'

'Ajar, half-open. Should we just peep in ?'

'I... I suppose we could. But it all feels a bit too silent and eery.' Shadows crowded round them.

'Do you think there might be something wrong?' said the rabbit quietly.

Emily didn't speak, but he could feel her ranging up, white fur bristling, tail stiffly waving.

'YOU'RE DEAD RIGHT RABBIT. THERE IS SOMETHING WRONG. FOR YOU AND THE CAT, THAT IS.'

A loud coarse voice had spoken behind them. Then, SMOOSH. Everything went dark for the Bottle Rabbit. Something soft and thick had been thrust over his head and strong claws clutched him. He kicked and struggled in the breathless dark.

'DON'T BUDGE ANOTHER INCH OR YOU'LL FEEL THIS IN YOUR BACKBONES,' and something hard prodded into his soft shoulders. The rabbit went still and felt himself being lifted, bundled along a few yards, then dumped on to what felt like a carpet. He heard whirring and hissing and a soft flump nearby. 'Must be Emily landing,' he thought.

'What are you doing to my friend?' he called, half angry, half afraid. Or tried to call. What came through the soft bag over his head sounded more like 'Woof oof yoof doofing.' And immediately a claw was clapped over the bag where his mouth was.

'IF YOU'LL BOTH SHUT UP AND KEEP STILL I'LL TAKE THE BAGS OFF. OK? The rabbit nodded his head hard.

'AND NOT BEFORE. OK?

Some animal was shaking him roughly. He nodded his head as hard as he could. He could hardly breathe in this appalling bag.

Then he gasped in relief. The bag had been dragged off and he could see and breathe again. What he first saw was beautiful Emily, all paws bound, white furry chest heaving. She was staring disdainfully in front of her. Then he saw their enemies: three gloved and masked ferret-desperadoes swaggering about with evil grins on their snouts. He and Emily had been dragged right into the badgers' aunt's once-tidy cottage home. No longer tidy. Everything upside down; drawers sagging open, a sofa with legs in the air, lace curtains drooping at the windows, a statuette stuck head-first in a plastic flowerpot, the aunt's treasured aspidistra broken-branched on the carpet. Worse still: in one corner of the sitting-room, propped against the wall, two unhappy badger-sisters lay bound and gagged, their brilliant eyes popping out of their heads.

'They wouldn't shut up. Especially that one,' the fat leading desperado muttered. He pointed a gloved paw at Dorothy.

'Oof oonfy Roonoof woof hoof,' she mumbled through her gag, a blue linen tea-towel with sprigs of rosemary on it.

The masked figures ignored Dorothy's mumble and turned their cold eyes on the rabbit. 'Tie him up,' snapped the fat one; and they tied the rabbit's front paws tight and tied his back paws tight, so he could hardly move.

'Gag?' queried the thin one, holding up another tea-towel.

'Not if he shuts up, not worth it,' growled the fat one, who was staring at the rabbit's black woolly chest. 'I'll have that, though,' he muttered, plucking the Magic Bottle from the rabbit's special front pocket. 'You've lost your bottle my friend. This'll come in handy, for milk. Right chaps?' A gross wink at his companions, who guffawed. The fat one smelt of whisky. The Bottle Rabbit was outraged. Mostly at the theft of his Bottle, but also because he hated jokes about it, especially silly puns about losing it.

Clearly a burglary was going on. Strewn about the room were lumpy sacks full of candlesticks, bits of jewellery, a sewing machine, silver spoons, watertight boots, wax candles, pots and pans, a tea canister (full), tins of baked beans, an eiderdown, several jars of home-made jam, odd pieces of fat. It was the burglars' swag.

Things now became quite nasty. The fat desperado picked up a heavy mallet and waved it in front of the two badgers.

'Where's the money? Where's the cash?' he kept

shouting. And he brought the mallet down THUMP just next to poor Dorothy's toes. Both badgers shook their heads fearfully and oonf oonfed, trying to say they hadn't any money.

'Take it easy, Bushy,' said the thin, masked desperado, 'No really rough stuff, not yet anyhow.'

'Why not?' Bushy plucked the gag from Margaret's trembling mouth.

'Suppose I start banging your talkative sister's little toes with this mallet? Perhaps you'd tell us where you keep your money then?' Eyes glinting through his mask, he lifted the mallet. Dorothy shrank into herself and Margaret bit her lips. But the two others held Bushy back.

'Knock it off, Bushy. We've got all their stuff. Let's take a break. What we need's a drink.'

'Good thinking, Bagot,' said the third desperado, whose name was Green.

'Look, Bushy, suppose you nip down to the grocer's and get some beer? There's lots of time. No one else is coming here tonight. We'll wait for you in the kitchen.'

Bushy, who was very fond of beer, thought it over. 'Yes. 'Myes. I might just do that. You two can pay, though.'

Green, looking annoyed, handed over some coins.

'See you later, then,' grunted Bushy. 'And you,' he glared at the shrinking Margaret, 'you'd better change your tune. Quick. Or else.' He stumped off, slamming the door. Bagot and Green nodded at one another, smirking and sidled off into the kitchen, leaving the four hapless animals alone.

Little did they know that plot and counterplot were being hatched among the treacherous villains. Bagot and Green had a plan to take Bushy's share of the swag.

Bushy had his own scheme to cheat them.

Green was muttering in the kitchen shadows:

'So it's agreed. When fatty gets back, you'll talk to him, Bagot. Talk about beer; he's always interested in that. And I'll creep up behind and bop him with the mallet. That'll put him out of action for half-an-hour or so. Gives us time to make a getaway with the swag. There's plenty of stuff in the sacks. Forget this money Bushy's got on the brain.' He chuckled evilly.

'Right,' muttered Bagot, 'I talk. You bop. Got it.'

'Then we're in business,' muttered Green. He swung the mallet back and forth.

'This'll keep him quiet for half-an-hour or so,' he said, to himself. 'He won't know what's hit him.' They both laughed.

Meanwhile at the grocer's Bushy, mask off, was buying a six-pack of bottled beer. Pausing only to gulp one beer down (and to throw the empty into a rose-bush) he clumped off in his leather riding boots to a chemist's shop. A young mouse advanced to serve the ferret.

'Look,' Bushy grunted in his surly way, 'I need some pills to put me to sleep for half-an-hour or so. Know what I mean?' He glared at the inoffensive little mouse-chemist.

'Well... ah... it's a bit irregular, sir, but I think I have something that'll serve your purpose very well. It's small white pills. They're tasteless, but very strong, extremely strong. They work fast; you must be extremely careful, sir'

'Give me two lots, then, quick. And when I want your advice I'll ask for it.' Bushy flung money down on the counter. The gentle mouse shook his head as he watched his customer lumber off, leaving the shop door wide open as he went.

On his way back Bushy stopped, opened three beer bottles, drank one fast (throwing the empty into a flowering azalea), then cunningly slipped a set of the white pills into each of the others. He closed them again, opened yet another bottle, gulped that down (throwing the empty over some animal's garden wall), and went on his way, chuckling evilly. 'These'll keep 'em quiet for half-an-hour or so,' he said to himself, 'They won't know what's hit 'em.' He laughed.

Soon, masked again, he was pushing in through the kitchen door.

'Here you are, chaps, come and get it,' he bawled, and held out the two doctored bottles.

'Brilliant, Bushy,' said Bagot. 'Great beer. And look what it says on the label; I think you've won some sort of prize.' Bushy, belching (he'd just opened the last bottle in the six-pack) leant forward to look. Green darted from the shadows behind him, swung his mallet, and - BOP - down it came on Bushy's bony head. He slumped to the ground, out cold. Beside him the last beer bottle spilled and splashed. The other two grinned at one another and opened their bottles.

'Good work, Green.'

'Here's to us, Bagot.'

They both swigged away thirstily.

In the other room four worried and puzzled animals had heard first a heavy Bop, then a heavy Thud and a Splash, and then slow heavy Breathing. Now they heard Swigging and Gulping sounds, followed by loud Yawns, then two more heavy Thuds and then more slow, heavy breathing. What was going on?

Snores began. Emily, who had been staring round the ravaged sitting-room, her cat's eyes gleaming dangerously, looked straight at the Bottle Rabbit.

'How very curious. I do believe they are all having a nap out there,' she whispered. 'Strange, but perhaps we can take advantage of the situation.'

'But what can we do?' quavered Margaret.

'Oof oony Roonooff woof hoof', came Dorothy's mumble again.

'What is all that oomfy Roonoof stuff?' whispered the Bottle Rabbit.

'I think she's saying 'If only Ranald were here,' whispered Margaret. 'Poor Dorothy'.

'Ranald?'

'It's her boy-friend, sort of. He's one of the Booges. A bass-player. Plays the cello at home. She adores him from afar.'

Emily, who'd been thinking, broke in quietly.

'Bottle Rabbit. Look. They've left your Magic Bottle up on that bamboo plant-stand over there. Do you think you might be able to roll over and over and get to it and shake that stand so the Bottle falls off? Perhaps you could then lie on the floor next to it and pongle from there? Pongle the General Alarum and get the Golden Eagle and start a rescue?'

'But what if my Magic Bottle gets smashed?'

'Well there is that ruched pouffe on the floor next to the plant-stand; that should break its fall.'

'Mn', whispered the rabbit worriedly. 'Oh, OK, then I'll have a go, I suppose.'

'It's our only chance,' whispered Emily, 'They might wake up at any moment.' All flinched as more loud snores came from the kitchen.

'Oh, do try,' whispered Margaret.

'If oony Roonooff...' began Dorothy. Emily looked the Bottle Rabbit firmly in the eye.

'I'll wriggle up beside you and help to push you and roll you,' she said out loud.

'Will you really, Emily? OK, then. Let's try,' whispered the rabbit.

So that is what they did. Together, cat and rabbit wriggled and pushed and rolled over, once, twice, three times on the fitted carpet. Then three more times. Then three more times again. It was hard going. Edging round the sacks the Bottle Rabbit banged into an occasional table and nearly got smothered by a pile of purple antimacassars that fell on him. Then he banged his head on a mahogany commode and barked his shins on a brass fender. At one point a large pot of artificial poppies splattered all over them both.

'How I wish we were still plunging in the water-meadow,' he whispered breathlessly to Emily, who was heaving and pushing beside him.

'Or dancing in the beech-grove,' she whispered back.

They were making progress, but it was slow work. Encouraging whispers came from Margaret, and an occasional 'oonf' from Dorothy. But now the kitchen-snorings were quietening down. Were the ferret-desperadoes going to wake up and ruin their plan? A fusee clock ticked heavily on the wall; fifteen minutes had gone by.

The two animals struggled bravely on. But then disaster struck. An abrupt movement brought a heavy oaken music stand toppling over and pinning them both to the carpet. They weren't hurt at all, but try as they would, panting and heaving, they couldn't budge this heavy stand one inch.

'Now what?' whispered the Bottle Rabbit, head

down against the dusty carpet. Emily sneezed and closed her eyes in worried thought.

'I'll tell you what,' piped a skinny little voice at the Bottle Rabbit's long left ear, 'I'll go and get the police for you; I'll go and get those bulldogs, Trevor and Howard.' The rabbit blinked. Pinned as he was he couldn't even see who was speaking.

'It's me, it's Maurice; surely you remember me? Maurice the ant?' The rabbit blinked again.

'Maurice? Maurice? Why, of course, yes, you're the kind ant who helped me when I was going North after my Magic Bottle. Yes, of course. How are you Maurice?'

'Very well indeed, thank you. Couldn't be better. I like this sunny late-June weather, don't you? It makes me feel all frisky and light-hearted and bright. A funny thing, though, my brother Albert doesn't like June at all, says it makes him...' The ant broke off. Emily was whispering urgently.

'I do believe you should leave instantly for the police station, Maurice. Those desperadoes might wake up at any moment.' The snores had grown much quieter n the kitchen; they could even make out a kind of broken sleepy muttering. 'Bop... gotcha... bop... beer.'

'Do hurry along to the station as fast as you can,' Emily urged. 'Speed is of the essence.'

'Right. Quite right. Desperadoes, are they? Well, we'll have our little talk another time,' said Maurice to the Bottle Rabbit, and the ant scurried off at an extraordinary rate. 'Won't take me long,' he called over his shoulder in his tiny voice.

Time passed. From the outside Sett House looked calm, tranquil even. But the sun's early evening rays shone through its lace-curtained windows onto two quite astonishing scenes. In the shambles that had once been their aunt's dainty sitting-room, two young badgers sat trussed up in a corner, one of them gagged. And a cat and a rabbit lay prone on the dusty fitted carpet, pinned down by a handsome oaken music stand. In the kitchen, three masked ferrets lay splayed on the tiles, groaning and rubbing their heads in their sleep, muttering odd things to themselves.. 'The label'.. 'Bop'.. 'This'll fix 'em'... 'Won't know what's hit 'em'... 'Mallet'... 'Bop'... 'Beer...' Legs twitched, claws clutched and unclutched. Plates of beans-on-toast, the badgergirls' tea, lay cold and untouched on the kitchen table.

Half-an-hour or so had gone by. Bagot and Green were stirring, clutching at their heads. They had terrible headaches from the sleeping pills. They woke up, squinted in each other's eyes, scowled horribly and, with one accord, scrambled painfully to their feet. Bushy still lay half-groaning, half-snoring on the tiles. Turning together, the other two strode and stumbled into the sitting-room. Cat, rabbit and one badger gasped: the other badger oonfed. But the desperadoes ignored them. They had only one aim, to pick up the swag and get away before fat Bushy woke. They were frightened of him.

They grabbed sack after sack of stolen goods and, cursing and stumbling, they opened the front door and flung each one clanking on the handcart outside. Back they came for the rest. Green turned and glared at the trapped Bottle Rabbit, muttering something about 'mallet' and 'bop'. But Bagot pushed him on.

'No time. Let's get out of here'.

The door slammed behind them and a key turned in the lock. Some hoarse laughter started up outside, then died away as suddenly as it had begun. A new, strong voice could be heard.

'All right, ' it was saying, 'You can stop laughing now. Stand still just where your are, and paws out. Right. We'll try these bracelets on for size.' Twice came a clatter of metal, and angry breathing.

'Handcuffs,' whispered Emily. 'Police. I think it's Trevor. Bravo Maurice.' The Bottle Rabbit shuddered for an instant, then whispered 'Hooray' weakly. But all was not over.

With a terrifying CRASH the kitchen door had swung open again, and there in the doorway, swaying and staggering, holding his bruised head with one hand and swinging a mallet in the other, was the third, worst desperado, muttering coarse words and staring brutally at them all. His mouth was full of cold beans-on-toast. His mask had slipped.

Margaret, dumbfounded, gave a badgery squeak.

'I know you. You're Bushy the ferret. I've met your sister, Molly.' This was a mistake. Bushy threw the mallet aside, leapt at Margaret, and in an instant had the poor tied-up badger over one shoulder.

'You'll do for a start. They won't take me while I've got you. And I'll have that Magic Bottle.' He pocketed it. 'There'll be a ransom to pay, too.' He glared round the room. 'I'll get the others later. Don't worry, I'll be coming for you one day, and with a mallet.'

After these awful words he clumped out through the kitchen, Margaret quivering on his shoulder. They heard the back door open, and bang shut.

'Oof oony Roonoof..' began Dorothy, eyes popping out of her head. But another familiar strong voice outside silenced her.

'What's all this then?' it was saying. 'I'll take that parcel you're carrying. I mean, I'll take that badger you're carrying. Also that Bottle. And I'll take you, too. Paws out. Right. We'll try these bracelets on for size.' More heavy breathings from outside the back door.

'It's handcuffs. Howard's caught Bushy,' cried Emily. 'Margaret's safe; we're all safe at last.' It was true, the animals' ordeal was suddenly at an end.

———

'Thank goodness you dropped in at the badgers' aunt's cottage, Maurice,' said Emily, some hours later.

'Yes. It's on one of my routes,' said the pleased ant.

'And thank goodness Trevor and Howard did so well,' said Fred. 'Say what you like, those police bull-dogs can be relied on in an emergency. Skillfull too, the way one went to the front door and the other to the back. Clever that.' Margaret nodded her head hard, and so did Charlie.

'What's come over the ferret world, though?' Fred went on. He and Charlie, Sam the Bear and Maud, Emily and the Bottle Rabbit, Dorothy and Margaret, and Maurice and Maurice's brother, Albert, were sitting over a very late high tea. In the end, Charlie had gone to the grocer's. There was ham, salad, beans-on-toast, cheese and pickled onions, followed by jelly and blanc-mange. Count Hubert was also sitting there, long past his bed-time, yawning away. Charlie had been helping him with his homework, sums mostly.

'I mean, first there was that Baxter, the accountant,' continued Fred, slowly munching his beans. 'Now it's these three, robbing and plundering, tying animals up, bopping one another. What's their trouble? Out of work are they? Short of money?'

'No, no, not at all,' said Sam. 'They all come from very respectable homes. And they all have perfectly good jobs. That's the strange thing. I believe one of them's even at the Bank. No, it's some strange new restlessness in the air. A mad search for excitement at any cost.'

'What'll happen to them?' asked the Bottle Rabbit. 'Will they be put in prison?' Count Hubert gave an agitated little sleepy squeak. Emily patted him gently on the head, took him off to bed, and told him a quiet story about a green pig.

'Prison you ask,' said Sam. 'And well you might. But I've had a word with the bulldogs and I think they may end up before the Ferrets' Board of Trustees. Yes. Those ferrets are like the Tiger Toms; they know how to deal with their own, how to ensure that nothing like this happens again. And I can assure you there will be adequate compensation for all concerned. I have a lot of time for our local ferrets. A fine body of animals, in every sense...' Sam continued talking for a while.

'Bushy said he'd come back and get us later,' quavered Margaret at a pause in Sam's speech. 'With a mallet. I'm frightened.'

'So am I,' quavered Dorothy. 'And the worst of it is, Ranald's off on tour with the Booges. I happen to know.'

'Now don't you worry,' said Fred, very kindly. 'Sam's right. Those three creatures won't dare to show their heads in this neck of the woods again. They know they'd be up to their ears in trouble if they did. The ferrets will be keeping a sharp eye on them, and keeping their noses to the grindstone. Especially that Bushy. Don't worry. Chins up.' The badgers calmed down. And so did the Bottle Rabbit.

So Friday evening ended cheerfully enough. Later on Howard and Trevor bicycled over in their off-duty brown suits, and were greeted with loud cries and

served beer and cheese. All animals chatted together until bedtime. The Bottle Rabbit tried hard to join in, but somehow he couldn't feel fully at ease until the two bulldogs were on their high machines again, boots pushing off, wheels going tick, tick, tick. It was true that Trevor and Howard had been brave and skillful and had saved them all, but then there'd been little Count Hubert. It was a puzzle.

By now the rabbit was also simply sleepy. Fred was drying the last dishes, Charlie was locking up. A big wood fire was crackling cheerfully in the cool of the late-June night, so he curled up near it, and Emily lay softly beside him, sleepily blinking at the flames. It was dark outside. The Bottle Rabbit dozed, his quiet mind slipping away from thoughts of deadly nightshade and desperadoes and bulldogs, easing closer to pennywort, pansies, purple loosestrife and slow, happy plunging in the water-meadow. Very soon he and all the other animals in Fred and Charlie's cabin were asleep, safe and sound in that warm, quiet place.

SATURDAY

The Cricket Match

The Bottle Rabbit got up early on Saturday morning. He'd slept well, in spite of Friday's wild goings-on. And he was looking forward like anything to the Cricket Match. Surely, he thought, that was going to be a calm, cheerful, unpuzzling affair.

Months ago, Hodge, the cricketing Tiger Toms' captain, had dropped in at Sam's for a cup of tea and then challenged the Foresters to a match. These lithe tom-cats were a keen lot, travelling widely for their sport, playing cricket every Saturday and most Wednesdays in the season. They practised hard too; Hodge was a stern taskmaster. And although they sometimes got a little too worked up about it all, they were a much-respected, well-liked group of sports-manlike cats. The Foresters, captained as always by Sam the Bear, had accepted their challenge, and a date had been set. It was late June, in fact the last Saturday in the month.

The Foresters usually played a dozen or so matches each summer, winning a few, losing a few. They were on the whole easy-going about their cricket. Yet although they never actually said anything, Fred and Charlie, and especially Sam the Bear really wanted to beat those Tiger Toms.

The Bottle Rabbit had just finished his porridge and boiled egg and was scraping up marmalade with bits of toast when Sam's dark bulk loomed in the bright doorway.

'Sam! What a lovely day! Perfect for the Match.'

'Yes, ' said Sam. 'Heavenly weather, really.'

'I hope I can keep the score right this time.'

'The score? Ah... yes. Yes of course. The score. But Bottle Rabbit, listen. We... yes, we want you to play today. Yes. We need you'.

'P-play?' stammered the astonished rabbit. He was blushing deeply.

'Yes. We've just received a message from Norman. The Golden Eagle flew it in as a matter of fact. I believe he missed breakfast in order to get here in time. Norman is still getting over the mumps, poor fellow. Great pity. He is a fine slip-fielder, that pigeon, and quite a useful bat too, on his day. But there it is. Yes. And at this late date there is, well, there is simply nobody else. And naturally of course we all of us think you a very promising young player yourself. Yes. So get changed and come right along and we will give you some practice.' Sam smiled benignly down.

The Bottle Rabbit was what you might call flabbergasted. Delighted but also scared stiff.

'Goodness, Sam. B-but what about... what about the scoreboard?'

'Don't worry, Bottle Rabbit, I'll take care of that,' murmured a gentle voice behind him. It was Emily, smiling and stretching in the sunny window.

'Will you really? But Emily, do you know how to?'

'Of *course* I know. I know how to play pretty well too, for that matter. I've knocked some of that tom-cat fast bowling about often enough at the cat-club nets,' said Emily firmly. It was true. Emily was a skillful cricketer, an all-rounder to boot. Sam would happily have included her in his team had she not been a cat herself.

There was a question of etiquette here.

'Well buck-up, Bottle Rabbit. Show them what you can do,' cried Emily in her go-to-it-ish sort of voice. And, bursting with happiness, the rabbit was soon marching off, bat in paw, his taut woolly body dressed in creamy white cricket flannels, clean white boots on his black paws. He had never played in a real cricket match before, with umpires and everything.

The Foresters Ground is a green meadow surrounded by dipping willows and broad oaks. In one corner of this lovely field is a Pavilion, with wrought-iron railings and benches and an old wooden score-board. In another corner, half ringed with limes and chestnuts, stands the ancient Red Lion Inn where you can sit, lemonade glass or beer mug in hand, and watch the cricket from long, weathered tables set outside. Fred and Charlie kept this ground's outfield well-mown, and a dozen young stoats volunteered every summer to clip and cut and water and roll the central strip.

At 2.30pm precisely, a gold bus rolled up to the Red Lion and out sprang the Tiger Toms, every manjack of them dressed to the nines in blue blazers and dazzling white flannels. Sam and Fred greeted them and led them into the Inn, where soon both teams, the two umpires and various friends were enjoying a hearty set meal, a late lunch of cold roast pork and artichokes, with baked beans for those who wanted them, all washed down with either lemonade or beer.

'Better not overdo this, eh Charlie,' said Fred, looking across his frothy pint of brown ale at his fellow-Clydesdale. Charlie grinned, swallowed a pickled egg, drained his pewter mug and passed it up for one more round.

At 3.30 it became time for cricket, and the Tiger Toms, having won the toss, elected to bat. All the benches round the Pavilion and the Red Lion Inn were now crowded, and cheerful animals, many with straw boaters or orange and yellow parasols, were dotted round the boundary. A murmur of interest went up as the two labrador umpires, Ralph and Lloyd, who had bicycled out especially from the town for this match, moved thoughtfully to the middle in their long white coats.

Sam led his team out to a scatter of applause, and he and his opening bowler, the big handsome mouse Geoffrey, began setting a field for Fritz and Felix, the Tiger Toms opening pair.

The Bottle Rabbit, proud in his white clothes but with heart pounding, was placed at deep fine leg, and he hopped off to his position, mostly hoping that the hard red leather cricket ball would never come his way. After his first happiness, worries had set in. He had been so tense about it all at lunch he'd only been able

60

to nibble at a little salad and down half a glass of pink lemonade.

Now the match got under way. The Tiger Toms batsmen began to hit out confidently at everything, but they were soon having their ups and downs. Felix's innings was typical: after a quiet start he quickly hit two crisp fours through the covers, and then tried for a third off a good length ball from Colonel Hare (of the Blue Hares) only to fall to a smart catch off the shoulder of his bat, taken by the little red squirrel Adlestrop, alert at second slip. Fifteen minutes play, seventeen on the board, one cat out. And so the game went. The Tiger Toms were in their over-eager mood. In too much of a hurry to score, they took big risks. So the careful bowling of Ambrose, Colonel Hare and especially Geoffrey took a steady toll.

Still, the cats were scoring plenty of runs. And both Hodge and Fritz, the latter a powerful batsman sporting a clerical collar, looked like staying there for a long time. Yet Geoffrey got them both in the end. And most of the others, cat by cat, lost their wickets to reckless strokes.

Four good catches were taken on the boundary by Fred and Charlie. Sam, when he saw how things were going, had wisely put them there to watch out for wild cat shots. Macavity, a devilish, rakehell of an animal, tried to hit his very first ball out of the ground for six. He almost did it, too, but couldn't quite make the length, and Fred was there on the boundary waiting under the trees. The big brown cart horse calmly took his curly pipe from his mouth with one hoof and caught the speeding ball in the other. That was the end of Macavity. Tom, Dick and Harry all went the same way, all tempted into giving catches in the deep field.

Only the great Fergus, a rangy, gingery creature with a crooked grin, who came in at 38 for 4, kept his head throughout. Driving, hooking and pulling the ball with remarkable accuracy, he provided a dazzling series of clean, diamond-cut strokes. Thanks largely to him the Toms ended up with a score of 101 (Fergus 52 not out), a big total in this kind of cricket. Loud and generous applause greeted Fergus as he and his last partner strolled back to the Pavilion.

It was now nearly 5 o'clock so tea was taken in the Pavilion. Two long tables set together, with long wooden forms on either side under the open shutters. Plates piled with cut bread and butter, cucumber sandwiches, mustard and cress sandwiches, and cake. At the top of the table stood an enormous urn of boiling water, three large brown teapots and an array of plain white cups. Slowly the animals crowded in through the swing door from the changing room, in the middle a breathless Bottle Rabbit.

He was glad the Tiger Toms innings was over. He had only made two real mistakes. Once, a fast ball from Geoffrey had come skidding down off de Selincourt's pads and bounced past him. Two leg-byes were scored off that one. The other mistake had been more serious. Fergus, at 26 had misjudged a leg-glide off the same bowler and given the only chance in his innings. The bright red ball came arching over towards the Bottle Rabbit, high and fast and hard. Yet it seemed to take an age to come down. At last he grabbed at it, only to feel it slip through his trembling grasp. A costly error. Subdued cries of relief came from knowledgeable older

cats in the Pavilion, and some murmurs of consterna-
tion among the Foresters supporters outside the Red
Lion. His team mates had all been terribly nice about it.
'Bad luck, old chap.' 'Hard lines'. 'Sun in his eyes you
know.' 'Jolly good try.' but the Bottle Rabbit knew the
truth. At tea he ate nothing.

Otherwise, the long tea interval proved a pleasant
enough event for both teams, with the Tiger Toms grinning and nodding and chatting. Yet there is always that
tense, withdrawn note about a cricketing tom cat, even
when he is merely handing round a plate of cucumber
sandwiches. Sam the Bear was well aware of this, and
kept a firm look on his face while exchanging small
jokes with Hodge and Fritz.

The Pavilion clock struck half past five. 'Yes. Our
turn to have a go,' rumbled Sam. Tea was being cleared
as Fred and Charlie, each of them puffing away on their
pipes, ambled out to open the Foresters innings in the
golden evening sun.

'Not going to be easy,' said Fred, quietly.

Charlie nodded. It was he who was taking first
knock, facing the dreaded Macavity, known
throughout the woods as a demon bowler. Charlie was
not in the least bothered at the sight of this rackety cat
tearing down the pitch and hurling that hard red
leather ball at the stumps and at him. Macavity was fast
but often inaccurate. Waiting for him the big cart horse
made a splendid figure, a faded blue and white club
cap on his head, old-fashioned brown pads on his
forelegs, his rumpled flannels held up by a green-and-
yellow striped tie rather than a belt. Charlie's tactics
were simply defensive. Every ball that was on the
wicket was blocked; everything else he let fly harm-
lessly by.

Fred, however, was soon playing a cheerfully adventurous game, using his bat like a broad mallet, and scoring quickly. His innings came to an early end, though, when he accidentally trod on his wicket as he made a huge pull to the fence, off a fastish rising ball from Fergus. But not before he'd smacked Macavity's bowling about a bit. That made it *12 for 1 (Fred 12)*.

And so the struggle went on, watched by a crowd that was growing noticeably more lively in front of the Red Lion. The Golden Baker scored freely off the luckless Macavity but was caught behind the wicket when he flicked at one of Fergus's fast out-swingers. The big mouse, Nigel, elegant in cream shirt and dark blue foulard, hit two neat singles and then was clean bowled by a Fergus yorker.

Now a long careful captain's innings from Sam the Bear produced ten runs in thirty-five minutes, all in singles. This slow pace (Charlie still wasn't scoring at all) brought cries of 'Get a move on out there' and 'Boring' and some loud yawns from the noisier cat element at the Inn. But Sam and Charlie played stolidly on and seemed to be there for good. Until Sam was smartly run out by de Selincourt, who had noticed that the dignified bear was sometimes slow to get moving after he had struck the ball.

The Foresters had now made *34 for 4 (Charlie not out 0)*, a dangerous but not impossible position. Time was passing, though, and for players and spectators alike the game had turned tense and exciting.

Each of the later batsmen did something, but nobody lasted long. Geoffrey, like Nigel, scampered nimbly between the wickets, as mice will, and then was bowled round his legs by Fergus. For a while the two Blue Hares put up a lively resistance, the Colonel especially punishing the slow bowling of Tobermory, an older, more heavily-built cat. But in the end Fergus got them both. Ambrose, a nice young beagle, missed a shooter from the same inspired bowler, and the red squirrel, Adlestrop, became Tobermory's only victim when he popped a slow off-break into the waiting paws of ... Fergus again. (What a splendid match that fierce animal was having.)

Things now looked bad for the Foresters. The score was *79 for 9*; they needed no less than *22 runs* to avoid defeat; Charlie still had not scored a single run; and the last animal in was ... the Bottle Rabbit.

He had been crouched quietly on a bench for an hour or more, padded-up and ready. His heart beat faster as the last wickets fell and his bat handle grew damp in his sweating paws. Now, as a roar went up from the Pavilion cats at Adlestrop's departure, he knew that he had to walk out there.

He stumbled down the Pavilion steps in his heavy pads and set off across the grass. Some encouraging claps came, but he heard nothing. He felt alone. Blood beat in his large ears. The sun was lower now, and long shadows stretched towards him from the high oak trees. Swallows dipped and swerved across the lawn-like field. Far away a cock called and called again, but otherwise everything was silent and still. He was lonely. The crowd in front of the Red Lion, sensing that the game had reached its climax, seemed caught in a fixed pose, mugs and glasses lifted. All talk stopped, though a quick ear might have caught an occasional soft:

'Two more lemonades please, Miss,' or

'One ginger-beer and large gin over here, Mary'.

Meanwhile the small animal padded softly and

65

worriedly towards the distant wicket.

When he got there he hardly noticed Charlie's welcoming nod and smile. Confident of getting a last quick victim, the Tiger Toms had all moved in and were crowding round, grim smiles on their flat heads, immense paws outstretched into which any ball must surely drop. The Bottle Rabbit could feel the eyes of the ten fieldsmen and the two umpires cruelly fixed upon him; all seemed eager to see him go.

There were three balls left in Tobermory's over. The Bottle Rabbit took guard, calling for '*middle-and-leg*' in a dry-throated bleat and glancing hopelessly about him. Tobermory came trundling up and a slow, high wavering ball came curving down towards the waiting rabbit. It was a simple 'donkey-drop', often a good way of getting a catch from beginners. The Tiger Toms moved forward as one cat, eager paws outstretched.

But the Bottle Rabbit simply stood still. Not a muscle moved as the ball bounced past his bat. Expecting a clatter of stumps, he thought all was over. But no... a dry thud in the wicket-keeper's gloves, a gasp from the crowd... and de Selincourt was tossing the ball back to the bowler.

Tobermory tried it again; and again the same thing happened. The Rabbit stood rigid; he simply could not get himself to play the ball at all. Again the ball missed the wicket. Dead silence all round the ground. Nothing stirred. In the Pavilion's tea-urn steam hissed. Someone cleared his throat. No one went and no one came.

Then Tobermory changed his tactics and the last ball of his over came down fast and fierce. It pitched short and leapt towards the Bottle Rabbit's woolly chest.

'Goodness,' he thought in a split second, 'it might hit me and crack my Magic Bottle.' (He carried it always and everywhere, and there it was, bulging in his special pocket).

So he put his weight on his back paw, raised his bat to his chest to protect the Bottle, felt the hard ball crack against the bat, and saw it drop still in front of him. A quick tomcat leapt forward and picked it up. 'Perfect defensive backstroke,' the rabbit heard him mutter as the fieldsmen changed ends. Another Tom nodded in agreement, 'Bit of a dark horse this one.'

'Horse?' the rabbit said to himself, puzzled, 'What can they mean?'

It was Charlie's turn again. Time was running out now, and in a last effort to dislodge the stubborn Clydesdale they had put on a new bowler, Eliot, a youthful, excitable animal. But Charlie's bat seemed to have grown wider and wider. He blocked Eliot's first fast delivery as patiently and calmly as he had been doing all afternoon and evening. Then the second ball somehow turned and struck Charlie quite painfully on the left front knee-cap.

'How's that?' cried the young Tom.

Ralph the umpire shook his head; Charlie puffed several times on his pipe, rubbed his knee, walked up and down and got a new, funny look in his eye. Eliot, rather put out, on his third ball slung down a full-toss. And to everybody's amazement Charlie, still looking irritable, opened his shoulders, and, using his bat like a mallet, bopped the ball as hard as he could high over square-leg's head. Higher and higher it rose above the fieldsmen, climbing high into the sky, beyond the next field, beyond the meadow-sweet and haycocks drying there, and dropped far out of sight. In the distance there came a crash and the sound of shattered glass and toppling masonry. Nearby came the clatter of happy clapping. A six for Charlie! At last he had scored.

Then it happened again. Eliot, properly flustered now, sent down another full-toss and Charlie, his pipe puffing clouds of blue smoke, treated it in exactly the same way. Another mighty mallet-blow, another crash, again the shattered glass and toppling masonry. Six more runs.

At the Red Lion there was pandemonium. Blue Hares were thronging and surging; rejoicing beavers were throwing themselves about abandonedly. Behind the Pavilion, happy mice were dancing together and embracing. At the score-board, a white cat bounded gracefully up and down.

Eliot was looking desperate. Hodge and Fergus slipped over and talked quietly with him for a moment, and the unhappy cat, really a very good bowler, shook himself and calmed down. His next ball came deadly straight and true, perfectly pitched at Charlie's middle stump. but Charlie without a moment's hesitation stepped forward and drove it smartly past mid-on for a sizzling four. Sixteen runs in three balls, the great carthorse was transformed. Eliot drew a deep breath and with a backward half-look over the shoulder hurled another fine ball, again perfectly pitched and with a dangerous curve to it. Now Charlie leaped yards out of his crease and drove it to the long-on boundary, near the Red Lion Inn sign. The stroke was just one flash of prancing white and yellow, with a crack that echoed round the ground and set the blackbirds flying. Four more runs. At the Inn, forest animals laughed and sang and cheered, even wept. A dozen stoats seemed to be dancing a conga there. Fred, seated at a front table, raised his huge beer mug in silent tribute to his friend.

Sam the Bear, however, still seemed bothered. And with some reason. Sam was looking at the Pavilion clock. Three minutes to seven. Three minutes to go. *99 for 9*. Three needed to win. Last animal in. Last over. The Bottle Rabbit now had to face the bowling. *And the deadly Fergus had once more taken up the ball*.

Fergus whispered something to his crony Macavity, who now raced up and crouched within a few feet of the shrinking Bottle Rabbit, his claws out, his yellow eyes staring unwinkingly. Meanwhile, swinging the ball from paw to paw the wild-eyed Fergus paced lithely back to make his long run-up.

'I've got to hit the ball this time,' the poor Bottle Rabbit said to himself, 'I've got to. Or I'm a goner for sure. Oh, if only there was a cricket-pongle. I know, I'll do my bedroom shot.'

(Night after night, lying in bed, playing an imaginary game, he had worked out a stroke in his head and played it over and over. Ball after imaginary ball would come flying down and the Bottle Rabbit would lean forward gracefully and, with a full and elegant follow-through, drive each one past cover-point for four perfect runs, to the applause of a large crowd). Now he was going to give it a try in real life.

Down pounded the real Fergus, flat head nodding and nodding, eyes glittering, scraggly body prancing in rangy muscular rhythm. The red ball flew down the green pitch straight at the Bottle Rabbit, who half shut his eyes, gritted his front teeth and played his bedroom stroke.

'All is over. This is the end,' he thought. Then willow met leather with a loud 'pock'. And 'Come on! Come on!' Charlie was shouting. 'Run, rabbit, Run!'

He opened his eyes wide. He couldn't see where the ball had gone, but he hopped up the pitch anyhow. Then before he had got half-way a great cry went up from the crowd. Charlie stopped in mid-pitch and actually hugged him.

'Wonderful, Bottle Rabbit! Lovely stroke! Never seen such a classic late-cut in all my days. You've won the match for us!'

The Bottle Rabbit had scored a boundary, four runs. The Pavilion clock struck seven and the match was done.

All round the ground, boaters and parasols flapped and flashed. Above the uproar, Sam the Bear called out, 'Yes. Hip, Hip, Hurrah for all the players,' in a firm voice. Charlie waggled his bat cheerfully as he and the

Bottle Rabbit marched back to the Pavilion. Various forest friends ran out and hoisted the puzzled but happy rabbit onto their shoulders and Fred strode up to hand Charlie a foaming mug of ale.

Amid the hubbub the Bottle Rabbit could hear especially firm clapping from all the tom cats, who were nothing if not sporting, though none of them looked very pleased. 'Told you he was a dark horse,' muttered that same puzzling cat as he slowly clapped. But when the Bottle Rabbit caught Fergus's eye, this fierce cricketer gave him a crooked grin and a large wink.

———————

Winners and losers celebrated at the Red Lion. Mountains of sausages, crates of lemonade, barrels of beer. There was singing.

Towards closing time the Bottle Rabbit sat quietly

with Emily at one end of the outside tables in the warm June night. Inside, led by Macavity, they were bellowing out a rowdy Australian song:

O the moon shone down on Mrs Porter,
And on her daughter.
They wash their feet in soda water.

The Bottle Rabbit sighed. He still had a puzzled look on his face. 'You know, Emily,' he said, chewing hungrily on a large sausage, 'I still can't quite believe it. I got that winning boundary. Me. I actually scored four runs.'

'Well it's true, you really did, Bottle Rabbit,' said Emily.

Some stoats now wandered over. 'Excuse us,' broke in one of them, 'Anyone seen that big pig, Dennis? He let me have seven to one on the Foresters this morning

when he heard you was playing; no offence. I plonked down a fiver, see?' 'Me too,' chorused other stoats gathering round.

Emily had in fact caught sight of the pig in question after the game. He was sidling along behind the Red Lion, smiling stiffly and clutching a Gladstone bag. Then he'd disappeared.

'You mean Ken the Pig, don't you? No, I'm afraid not.' Emily looked a bit pink as she said this.

The fed-up stoats moved off, muttering. One of them, a thin-lipped animal called Flash Harry, made some rude-sounding noises.

'Really, Ken is the limit,' said Emily quietly. She was still a bit pink. 'He was here, you know. Fancy him taking those stoats' money, their bets, and then slinking off and not paying up when they won. I mean, I'm not all that keen on gambling getting into cricket. Still, my Uncle Edgar always used to say a bit of a flutter never did anyone any harm... Oh Well.' Emily shook her head and smiled, 'Sam will speak to Ken I'm sure.' They sat on.

'I didn't know you had an Uncle Edgar. You know it was all sort of an accident, really, that shot, Emily. I meant to do my special private stroke, my bedroom shot. But the ball hit my bat so hard it sort of twisted sideways and the ball went off behind me. I didn't even know where it had gone.'

'Never mind. Those were four good and valuable runs Bottle Rabbit.'

He swallowed some more sausage. 'But Charlie said it was a classic late-cut, whatever that is. He told me so. I've never heard Charlie talk so much about anything, ever.'

Emily smiled but did not speak. Things had grown

quieter. The Tiger Toms had gone off cheerfully enough in their bus and Nigel and Geoffrey could now be heard singing a gentle duet:

The moon hath raised her lamp above
To light the way to thee my love.

Cat and rabbit listened together for a while. At last the Bottle Rabbit spoke again. 'Fergus knew. He winked at me. I saw him.' The rabbit picked up another big sausage and gave another quiet little sigh.

'Listen, Bottle Rabbit,' said Emily firmly, 'Be sensible. All right, you dropped a catch.' The rabbit winced. 'All right, but you made up for it. All right, it wasn't the exact stroke you intended. But you scored the runs we needed. I thought it was a lovely stroke.' With that, Emily put her elegant white paw on the rabbit's woolly black paw.

The Bottle Rabbit, who was really thinking just the same thing, smiled sleepily as Emily's graceful white tail swung slowly in time to Nigel and Geoffrey's beautiful chant.

Pretty soon, tired but happy, all the animals were moving slowly home through the moonlit forest to their peaceful beds.

———

Extracts from *The Forest Echo*, July 2nd
Tiger Toms v. The Foresters
Match played at the Foresters Ground

PONGLE!

Tiger Toms

Rev. Fritz b. Geoffrey	13
Felix c. Adlestrop b. Colonel Hare	8
Macavity c. Fred b. Geoffrey	0
Hodge (Capt.) b. Geoffrey	15
de Selincourt lbw. b. Ambrose	4
Fergus not out	52
Tobermory b. Ambrose	0
Tom c. Charlie b. Geoffrey	2
Dick c. Fred b. Colonel Hare	3
Harry c. Charlie b. Geoffrey	2
T.S. Eliot b. Ambrose	0
Extras	2
Total	101

Bowling: Geoffrey 5-37, Col Hare 2-29,
Ambrose 2.24, Adlestrop 0-9

Foresters

Charlie not out	20
Fred hit wkt. b Fergus	12
The Golden Baker c. de Selincourt	10
Nigel b. Fergus	2
Sam the Bear run out	10
Geoffrey b. Fergus	7
Colonel Hare c. Felix b. Fergus	14
Sergeant Hare lbw. b. Fergus	10
Ambrose c. Tom b. Fergus	7
Adlestrop c. Fergus b. Tobermory	7
Bottle Rabbit not out.	4
Extras	0
Total (for 9 wickets)	103

Bowling: Macavity 0-33, Fergus 7-29,
Tobermory 1-21, Eliot 0-20.

The Foresters won by one wicket
Cat of the Match: Fergus
Horse of the Match: Charlie

SUNDAY

Three-Pongle Magic

The Bottle Rabbit woke very late next morning, tired out from the cricket and the party afterwards. He lay half-dozing, until he remembered last Wednesday's idea about doing a Sunday three-pongler with Emily. He clambered up, yawning and stretching. He'd missed breakfast, the two Clydesdales had already been at work on a Sunday job for hours, and Emily was long gone. So, pausing only to gulp a mug-full of milk, he hopped off towards that cat's forest home.

Before long he was standing in front of a certain great beech tree. Making a fist of his paw, he knocked on it three times. Paw on wood made a soft thud, and a door opened in the tree. Emily was standing there smiling. Behind her you could see a dining room and a drawing room with a fireplace, plates on the wall, buckets of coal, teapots and family portraits.

The rabbit, now wide awake, looked straight at the cat.

'White rabbits, white rabbits,' he said quickly. Emily laughed a lot.

'Well, you're not a white rabbit. But yes, it is the first of the month, July the first. So you get a private wish. Come in and make it in comfort.'

Inside he found Count Hubert sitting on the sofa counting the buttons on Emily's upholstery. The little rabbit nodded briefly, his lips moving rapidly, as the

Bottle Rabbit sat down beside him.

'Go ahead and wish,' said Emily, so he shut his eyes and, kind-hearted animal that he was, wished that Emily would get a surprise present as soon as possible. Hardly had he opened his eyes again when, amazingly,

a postweasel came skipping up to the door clutching a fair-sized parcel.

'Afternoon miss, special delivery for you.'

Emily, who loved parcels and packages, smiled all over her white cat's face. She signed for this one, said 'Thank you George' to the postweasel and began nimbly undoing the string. There was lots and lots of string. When she'd got it all undone she found inside a beautiful ring shaped out of beaten silver. There was a message with it:

We the assembled Ferret Trustees wish to say how sorry we are that you were put in a sack and bothered last Friday by three of ours who have brought shame to the ferret world. We therefore beg you to accept this present from the Trustees by way of apology and it won't happen again believe us if they know what's good for them. Also please read what it says on the ring.

For and on behalf of the Ferret Trustees,
Signed,
Egbert, Secretary and Carpenter

'Well,' said Emily, 'I wasn't put in a sack, just had a bag put on my head for a bit, and got tied up. But still, how very thoughtful.' She put the ring on and looked closely.

'It says here, "Twist me round three times and see what you hear."' She began.

'How can she see what she hears?' whispered Count Hubert. But music was filling the room and Emily was listening carefully.

'It's a trio, a string trio - one of Purcell's,' she purred. 'What a wonderful present. Now I can have music wherever I go.' The Bottle Rabbit turned to Count Hubert.

'Hubert, with music you can often see what you hear.' He paused. 'And, er, sometimes you can hear what you see.'

'Well all right,' said the little animal blinking, 'but guess what. I got a present from the ferrets this morning, too; because of Baxter and my bike. It's a thing you put on the wheel to count the miles. It's lovely. My Uncle Emsworth put it on for me. I can use it whenever I get a bit tired from counting them myself.' Cat and larger rabbit smiled and patted him on the head.

The Bottle Rabbit had gone a bit quiet. He couldn't help wondering whether he was going to get a present too. Then Emily remarked:

'Look, here comes George again.' The postweasel was panting and scrambling back with another fair-sized parcel.

'Afternoon, sir. Silly old me. Should have given you this in the first place. You are the Bottle Rabbit, aren't you?'

'I, er, well yes, I am,' said the Rabbit.

'Saw you yesterday at the cricket. Nice job. Sign here please.'

The delighted rabbit signed and began fiddling with the string and brown paper on his parcel. In the end Emily helped him with the string. His present turned out to be a handsome silver watch and chain, a half-hunter. With it was a similar ferret-message, the same being put in a sack and everything, but in his case it ended, 'Press the button three times and see what you hear.' He pressed the button three times:

'Ping Ping Ping: Continuing sunny and warm with temperatures in the high sixties. Forecast for tomorrow some early drizzle turning into heavy rain with patches of fog in the Midlands. Outlook for Tuesday, unsettled. Goodbye,' said the watch. The Bottle Rabbit was over-joyed.

'It's a weather-watch! I can get the weather when-ever I want it.' He slipped it into his other pocket.

'Could you see what you heard that time then?' asked Count Hubert.

'Oh shush,' said cat and rabbit, both speaking at

once, but in a kindly tone.

Emily served a very late, very good Sunday lunch. It was roast beef with Brussels sprouts, haricot beans, Yorkshire pudding, followed by treacle tart with lashings of cream. Count Hubert, who never ate meat, took extra vegetables and extra pudding. Afterwards they went out into the glade behind Emily's tree-house, the Bottle Rabbit pongled up some lemonade, and they all sat talking and laughing quietly in the warm sun.

General yawning began.

'A snoozelet, everyone?' suggested Emily. So they stretched out in the sunlit glade. The Bottle Rabbit was glancing at his new watch.

'Why, it's exactly 3:33,' he yawned. 'Perhaps I should do that three-pongle now.'

The other two nodded drowsily as he shook his Magic Bottle and 'Pongle' 'Pongle' 'Pongle'.

———

Nothing happened for a while as the animals dozed and yawned. Nothing, that is, until a battering clatter of loud trumpets announced a procession of brilliantly clad creatures, in scarlet silks, white satins and cloth-of-gold. Three antelopes led this procession. They halted in front of the rabbit and bowed their heads low. 'Good day, my lord. Good day, Baron Rabbit. Please to seat yourself upon this throne.' An antelope waved a hoof and three lions strode up carrying an ebony throne.

'Please to seat yourself, Baron,' said the antelope. The rabbit did so, and three powdered footmice in knee breeches ranged themselves behind him. Now an antelope was addressing his white cat friend:

'Please to seat yourself, Princess Emilia.' And the cat

was soon sitting in dignity on an ivory throne born up by three lionesses. She was wearing a high, glittering tiara. Behind her ranged three handmice, each wearing her own small tiara. Footmice and handmice handed goblets of nectar to the cat and the rabbit.

Now the three antelopes approached and sang in three-part harmony:

> You have now three hours,
> Three wishes are yours,

they chanted, nodding their heads and waving their horns.

'Do we have three wishes each?' asked the rabbit. The antelope nodded,

> Your three-pongle Fête
> Comes but once a year.
> So now please to make
> Your three wishes clear.

The rabbit emptied his goblet and looked perkily over at the cat. 'You go first.' 'Very well,' said the cat. She smiled a half-hidden cat-smile and turned to the antelopes.

'First I wish for a bobsleigh ride with my friend from the very top of an icy mountain to the very bottom.' An antelope bowed.

'Of course, your Majesty. From icy peak to snowy base.' He signalled behind him with a hoof.

Within three seconds the two animals had been swept up to a snowy summit. Sun blazed down on crackling ice and crisp snow. Up there more antelopes

were waiting, standing against the blue sky. Helmets and heavy clothing were handed out, and an antelope held the white cat's tiara for her, as she was going to steer. The intrepid cat flung herself onto a blue-and-white sleigh and the rabbit climbed carefully after her.

'Hold on tight,' she called as an antelope pushed them off.

And away they sped at

startling speed, racing headlong down a runway, the cat handling the bends and turns with astonishing skill. The only sounds in the silent snow were the hiss of steel runners on hard ice and an occasional gulp from the rabbit. It was the fastest he'd ever been in his life; three hundred miles an hour at least, he thought.

A last plunge down a towering ravine and they were on flat snow, racing towards more waiting antelopes.

'A goblet of hot nectar?' they asked as she leapt and he climbed slowly off the sleigh.

'Thank you, yes,' said the cat.

'Yes please,' gasped the rabbit.

'What a marvellous first wish!' said the cat, sipping daintily.

'Yes,' said the rabbit, in between hefty gulps.

———

Now they were back on their thrones.

'Right. I've thought of something,' said the rabbit. 'My first wish is... well... I want to have a quiet ride with my friend in a hot-air balloon. Not too high up though.'

'A balloon? Certainly my lord,' said an antelope, signalling with a hoof.

Within three seconds, cat and rabbit were whisked to a woodland hillside where a nine-animal hot-air balloon was poised to take off. It was a handsome vehicle, with elegant woodwork, plenty of shining brass, and great blue-and-white gores on its envelope. The seven-hen crew had already dealt with their splosh and were ready to go. 'All aboard,' clucked their captain, and the two guests were discreetly hoisted up.

'I suppose it's perfectly safe,' breathed the cat,

glancing up at the valve-line flapping over their heads. 'Oh, I'm sure it is,' muttered the rabbit, staring down at his back paws and gripping the side of the basket tightly with his front paws.

'Let go,' cried a hen; and with a Whoosh up they shot, the two animals clutching at one another a little.

'I could do with another goblet of that nectar,' whispered the rabbit.

'Nectar? Certainly my lord,' clucked a hen-assistant, who managed to hold on to a hoop with one foot and hand them each a goblet of nectar with the other. The two passengers gulped. By now they had stopped climbing, the basket had stopped swaying, and they were high above the woods and fields. They were actually moving quite fast, but there was no sense of movement. In fact, the earth below seemed to be moving slowly past *them*. It was lovely and quiet, though they

could just hear a dog barking far below. The only other sound was an occasional creak from the basket when a hen moved abruptly to obey an order.

The balloon was over woods now, and had come down quite a bit lower ('Cooler air; down draft,' an intelligent-looking hen said to the cat), and a new sweet and beautiful sound came to their ears. It was the combined singing of thousands of birds, of half the birds that make the forest summer so lovely - all blended together in wonderful harmony.

'Listen, I can hear wrens and chaffinches and black-birds and thrushes.'

'Yes. And I can hear hedge-sparrows and warblers and greenfinches and bullfinches, and I think a greater spotted woodpecker.' The cat gently punched the rabbit.

'You're showing off,' she murmured.

The ride ended as they came gently to earth in a water-meadow. 'Did you enjoy that?' asked the rabbit. 'Quite delightful,' said the cat. The rabbit had liked it a lot himself, but was also glad to be back on firm ground again.

Antelopes were waiting, and whirled them off in a gold and silver chariot towards their next wish. They passed through two marvellously-carved gates of horn into an ivory city where the chariot came to rest in front of a marble hall. The antelopes cocked their heads inquiringly:

> One wish each you've had,
> There are two more to go.
> Perhaps you'd be glad
> To see some some sort of Show?

they chanted.

'A show? Yes, what a very good idea,' said the white cat. 'I'd love to take the rabbit with me to a Flower Show. That's my second wish. I'm sure he likes flowers and plants as much as I do.'

'Yes, please, perfect,' said the rabbit, glad that it wasn't going to be another high-speed affair.

Within three seconds they had entered an enormous Conservatory, built of wrought-iron and glass, with a

roof so high that whole trees could fit in. The masses of flowers were a pleasant mixture of the strange and tropical, like purple orchids and hibiscus, and the familiar and local, like buttercups and daisies.

The two animals pottered along happily. 'Have you noticed,' remarked the cat, 'that they've given everything its old-fashioned name?'

'Yes,' said the rabbit, 'And have you noticed how many plants have animals' names?'

'So they have; let's see how many we can find.'

The rabbit looked round. 'Well, there's a horse-chestnut tree over there for a start.'

'And there's tiger-lilies here,' responded the cat.

'And Toad lilies.'

'Zebra plant.'

'Gooseberry bush.'

'Elephant bush.'

They began to speed up.

'Foxglove.' 'Harebell.' 'Duckweed.' 'Dogwood.' 'Cowslip.' 'Sheep Laurel.' 'Snake bush.' 'Spider fern.' 'Spider?' 'Oh, all right, Flea-bane, then.' For a moment they seemed to have run out of animals; then,

'Squirrel-tail trees,' said the cat.

'Goat's head,' said the rabbit.

'Cock's tail.'

'Lizard's tail.'

'Lamb's tongue.'

'Owl eyes.'

'Rabbit's ears. Bunnies' ears,' laughed the cat.

'Cat's ears. Cat's claws. Cat's whiskers,' cried the rabbit.

They both laughed a lot.

'You know, this all reminds me of a tumbling game I play sometimes, with my best friend,' mused the rabbit.

'Me too,' said the cat, in a soft voice.

Now they came to the great glass exit doors.

'What were your absolutely favourite flowers in the whole Show?' the rabbit asked as they prepared to leave.

'Well, I think Snow-on-the-Mountain and Snow-in-Summer. They both reminded me of that wonderful bobsleighing. What about you?'

'Patience and Honesty,' the rabbit replied.

'Oh, very good,' said the cat, smiling at him. 'Well, now it's time for your Show.'

As they walked out of the Conservatory, a small sprightly rabbit bounded past them. His whole body was painted in blue-and-white stripes. The little animal seemed to be counting the stripes to himself as he went along. He looked very happy.

———

The antelopes were back.

'And what Show would please you, my lord?' they asked in chorus.

'Oh. Er. Yes. Me again,' said the rabbit. 'Well... I'll... I think I'd like to... I've never ever been to a Circus. Could we go to the Circus? My friend and me, I mean?

Yes. That's my next wish.'

Three antelopes waved hooves and horns, and within three seconds rabbit and cat were seated in a red-plush box under a huge, taut circus tent lit by flashing limelight. The Big Top was full of noise and bustle and the blare of brass-band music. it was a three-ring circus, so wherever they looked something interesting was going on.

Lions and tigers prowled; elephants thumped about. A chimpanzee called Buffo the Great led a troupe of white-faced clowns, gambolling and leaping and jumping and calling out comical things. A pack of smiling Palomino horses galloped round the outer ring with marmosets spinning and twisting on their backs. In the second ring a team of armadillos was dancing, all raising their knees and singing loudly. One of them, especially agile, waved a sequined handbag as she danced. In the centre stood the ring-master, a majestic

Polar Bear with a slight lisp.

'Amuthe your-thelves,' he would call out, 'animalth mutht be amuthed.' Round him flocked a team of twelve stoat-tumblers who juggled as they tumbled. The cat and the rabbit sat entranced.

Far above stretched the fearsome-looking high wire and trapezes, all occupied

by happy monkeys. As they stared up, one of these monkeys leapt across the void and did a triple-somer-sault in mid-air before reaching the paw of a fellow-acrobat stretched out from his trapeze. The two visitors gasped.

'We call this the Happiness Circus,' chanted the antelopes standing behind their guests.

Things got more surprising. Suddenly one amazing young monkey who'd been jiggling about near them leapt from the circus floor to catch a dangling trapeze. She had jumped up thirty-three feet in a single bound, transfixed the while on the arching white sword of the limelight. An amazing scene; how could she do it? The rabbit was watching her through his opera-glasses.

'Phew! I wish I could do that,' he gasped. Then: 'Ooops!'

In three seconds, he had leapt high into the air, shot up to the dizzying trapeze, and was dangling next to the smiling monkey. He looked down without fear at the shining up-turned faces far below.

'Well done,' breathed the monkey as they swung back and forth, 'And now shall we go down again?'

The rabbit nodded, and with a leap, the two of them hurtled through the air, plummeting down to land lightly in the red-plush box next to an applauding white cat. The Big Top rocked with cheers and laughter. The rabbit stood with the monkey to acknowledge the applause. Meanwhile antelopes were chanting behind him:

> Don't worry my lord,
> That leap won't be reckoned
> As the last of your wishes
> But as part of your second.

When it came time to leave, cheers from circus animals followed the party's procession out of the tent.

———————

Once outside the antelopes chanted again:

> Before your third wish
> We've a show of our own.
> Come sit by this chasm
> Take each your high Throne.

'Did they say chasm?' whispered the rabbit. 'I think so,' the cat whispered back. Meanwhile they were being whirled away to the very edge of a deep chasm. Within three seconds they were installed on bronze thrones placed on that plunging edge. Antelopes chanted:

> Peer down in the depths
> And much evil you'll find.
> Bad creatures lurk down there,
> Unclean and unkind.

Keen and alert, they peered into the gaping chasm, smoke-laden, murky. Strange weak cries rose from its depths. Things bulked and loomed and fluttered down there. The rabbit suddenly stirred on his throne.

'Look! he shouted, 'It's the Crad; I'm sure it is.'

A 'Crark' floated up from below as a large gaunt bird appeared, its dusty black wings creaking, its hectic red eyes blinking and blinking.

'Crark, Crark, Crark,' it mouthed. The cat leant forward.

'Yes. It's the Crad all right. I think I can even catch a whiff of bread-crumby waistcoats down there, too.'

'So can I,' said the rabbit, wrinkling his nose. 'And stale flower-vase water. Wait a minute,' he peered down again. 'I do believe there's lots of them there. Look, there's lots and lots of Crads.' And sure enough, Crad after Crad rose slowly and clumsily into view.

'Crark. Crark. Crark.' Ragged claws outstretched. Beaks twisted. The Crads scowled and shook their pear-shaped heads each with its bald spot on top.

'I never thought there'd be other Crads. More than the one I've met already,' said the rabbit.

'And they all look as nasty as that one did. Do you think they're coming up here?'

But the antelopes were chanting reassuringly:

> They are far, far away,
> They can never get near.
> So there's no need to worry,
> There's nothing to fear.

The cat now drew in her breath.

'Good gracious, look over there. Surely that's the Grumble, up from his watery den?'

In the darkest parts a huge shapeless sort of Thing was stumbling about, clutching a gnawed raw fish in one great claw and a half-empty demi-john of rum in the other. They could just catch his faint roaring: 'I'm hungry. Where's that rabbit for my cooking pot? Where's that confounded white cat? Merritt! Get in here! I want my dinner! I want it now!'

The rabbit instinctively reached into his front pocket for his Magic Bottle, but antelopes calmed him again, chanting:

> He's far, far away,
> He can never get near.

91

So there's no need to worry,
There's nothing to fear.

'I suppose the Merritt must be down there some-where too,' said the white cat with distaste. As she spoke, a tiny moustached head peered from behind the Grumble's knee.

'Come on Grumb'. Give us a gulp,' it said in a reedy voice; skinny legs moved weakly beneath it. The Grumble just swiped at the creature with his rum bottle. Then dark clouds swept over both of them and they disappeared.

The rabbit was looking thoughtful.

'I think I see what the antelopes are doing,' he said. 'They're showing me the creatures who've bothered me so much in the past, but it's all perfectly safe here.'

'Exactly, me too' agreed the cat. 'It's a sort of Happy Nightmare. Quiet an interesting idea, enjoyable even. But I think we've seen enough, don't you? Especially after that Merritt.'

'Yes,' agreed the rabbit. 'He really is the worst of them all. Though the Grumble is much smellier; and so are the Crads. And Bushy stank quite a bit on Friday when he got close.'

Antelopes approached once more:

There's lots more to see,
There's a Rat and a Ram.
Three ferrets are down there,
And Grumble's old Dam.

'Oh thank you, but no, dear antelopes,' said the cat. 'That's quite enough for one day. Besides I've got an idea for my last wish.'

Without a moment's delay they were whisked back to their ebony and ivory thrones. And again the antelopes were chanting:

> You've now had two wishes,
> Feel perfectly free
> To tell us your third one.
> Please, what shall it be?

The cat smiled: I've just thought of one other flower at the Show, an orchid called Lady of the Night. It gave me an idea for my third wish. I wish..' The cat blushed a deep red, 'I want to be an opera star... Just for a few minutes.. I want to sing the Queen of the Night's great aria from *The Magic Flute*.

Within three seconds the rabbit found himself in another red-plush box, now in a magnificent Opera House, full of eager animals. Floating onto the stage came the white cat in a red gown and black high heels, singing her heart out. Long, lovely music. Up and down, low and high went the notes. It was like listening to a brilliant acrobat. The marvellous song

ended to a storm of applause, and as the cat stood there curtseying she was pelted with soft red roses from every corner of the great hall.

At last she was allowed to leave the stage, and the rabbit slipped round to meet her behind the scenes. She was radiant and surrounded by antelopes.

'That was wonderful,' he

cried, 'I wish I could sing like that.'

'Any particular kind of music, Baron?' It was the antelope yet again.

'Oh, er, I didn't really mean... oh, well, I do like Country and Western.'

'Certainly my lord. Your third wish shall be instantly fulfilled.'

Within three seconds the rabbit found himself on an open-air stage facing a buzzing crowd. There must have been three thousand rabbits there, all in check shirts, shoe-string ties, blue jeans and high leather boots. A delicious smell of hot-dogs, hamburgers, and chilli sauce wafted up to him. He too was wearing a check shirt, jeans and boots, and also a ten-gallon hat that kept slipping down over his ears.

A grizzled rabbit handed him a guitar.

'Howdy pardner. This here's your geetar, I reckon. And what you-all have in back of you is the greatest little old back-up group in three counties. That right, boys?'

'Sure is right,' said flat voices behind him.

Looking round the rabbit saw two big, oldish, palefaced, paunchy rabbits in the usual clothes, with guitar and banjo; a third little old rabbit held a battered violin. They nodded to him, blank-faced. The grizzled rabbit spoke again, 'Well, pardner, what are you-all fixin' to sing for those good old boys down there today?'

'Well, I thought I'd have a go at *The Blizzard*.'

'*The Blizzard*, you say? Well that's mighty fine. That's a mighty fine number in my book. It's a kind of a noble number.'

As the back-up swung into the melody of *The Blizzard*, three thousand rabbits began to cheer, then fell silent. Against the rough, scrawny tones of the country fiddle, the rabbit was belting out his ballad in a high tenor that sent shivers down every animal's spine. It was a very sad song about this cowrabbit riding thrice three miles home to his Mary-Ann on this much-loved old ill mule through a terrible snow storm. They'd struggled to within sight of Mary-Ann's cabin, but because of the weather could go no further. The audience was hanging on the singer's every word, and when he came to the part about yes, they found him on the plains with his paws froze to the reins, you could see tears streaming down the most hard-bitten rabbit's cheeks. Some sobbed openly. And at the last heartbreaking line, 'They were only a hundred yards from Mary-Ann,' there was first stricken silence, then roar upon roar of applause.

They made him sing the whole thing through again. More roars, then cries of 'Speech! Speech!'

'Thank you, thank you,' said the rabbit, 'I thank you very much. Thank you.'

'Speech!' they continued to roar.

'Well... I... erm...' said the rabbit, who had never made a speech in his life. He stared out at the massed rabbit faces. In one corner he noticed the white cat, smiling gently. She was laughing a bit. Was there something funny about his hat, he wondered. (It had happened to him before with hats.)

'Well... erm... I' he was beginning to say, when slowly all the rabbits' faces began fading away, everything grew quiet, and after one last distant wave from an antelope's hoof, he found himself staring across the glade at a beautiful white cat who was smiling gently, even laughing a bit, back at him.

———

The rabbit looked at his new watch. It was 6.33. Then he spoke to the cat.

'Princess Emilia,' he said.

'Yes, Baron,' She replied.

> '??????'
> '!!!!!!!!!'
> '??????'

'I've just had a most amazingly lovely afternoon,' they both said, both talking at once. Then they couldn't stop talking and couldn't stop laughing: 'Was that you?'

'Was that me?'

'Remember this?'

'Remember that?'

'What about this?'

'What about that' for a long time.

'So what did you like best of all?' asked Emily, finally.

'Well *The Blizzard* was sort of special, but I suppose I liked most that jump at the Circus and not being afraid,' said the Bottle Rabbit.

'It was brilliant', said Emily, 'But I must say I did love the Mozart.'

'The what? asked the rabbit. Was that a single red

rose petal he could see on Emily's right shoulder?

Then a scuffling interruption came. Count Hubert was standing between them, bright-eyed.

'I've just been at a lovely place,' he said excitedly. 'I was striped blue-and-white all over. It was lovely. I counted all the stripes. And they called me Viscount Hubert. And everybody liked me.' Was that a little blue stripe on Hubert's round stomach? The Bottle Rabbit shook his head wonderingly.

'Think of me up in a balloon,' he said to Emily.

'And just think of me steering a bobsleigh,' she replied.

'Do you think there really are lots of other Crads?' asked the Bottle Rabbit, on a different note.

'There might well be,' said Emily, very quietly. 'Ugh, what a horrible idea'.

'Yes. More of a Moanday idea, as Pob would say...'

'Is Moanday tomorrow; better have nice time today.' And little Pob himself was standing there in the glade, twirling his high hat and beaming at them. 'You come my house, eat some chairs?' (Pob's house was of course full of edible furniture). 'And very good new milk chocolate sofa just come in. Oh yes. Some parts full of coffee-cream. I think the legs.'

So they all trooped off to end that extraordinary magical Sunday enjoying Pob's hospitality in the Township of Yes.

———

It was dark when they got back to Fred and Charlie's, so Emily stayed the night. In answer to the cart-horses' kindly enquiries, they tried to explain about their three-pongle adventures, but somehow it was all too hard. So everybody went to bed fairly early, snuggling down warm and happy, gathering strength for Monday morning. That night Bottle Rabbit, Emily and Count Hubert all had lovely, happy dreams, about antelopes for some strange reason.

Kidnapped

It was Monday morning, and raining. In the woods disconsolate animals were ambling off to work, or off to school, but the Bottle Rabbit was just pottering along nowhere special. All through breakfast he hadn't been able to stop wondering about Sunday's three-pongle mysteries. But now he was wandering through the trees and thinking back to Saturday's cricket. He couldn't stop smiling about that. 'Four runs,' he murmured to himself, 'Bottle Rabbit... not out... 4.' and almost every animal he met seemed either to have been at the match or to have heard of it. 'Good work, lad,' called out a beaver, padding along with his case of barber's scissors and combs. 'Hope you're playing next time,' cried a hedge-hog from under her yellow-and-black striped umbrella.

The Bottle Rabbit's smile grew broader and broader. 'Well done,' said a matronly spaniel, as she pushed some young ones in a pram; it was a four-wheeled vehicle of iron and of wood, it had a leather apron, but it hadn't any hood. One old badger named Dobinson stopped and slapped him hard on the back (quite hard).

'Splendid. Splendid my boy. That late-cut of yours quite took me back. Reminded me of an innings of mine in '37, or was it '38? No, it was the year the woolly bears set up camp in the water-meadow. Must have been '37.' And Dobinson stood under his umbrella to tell him a long, difficult story about cricket that the rabbit didn't understand. As he was not under the umbrella, he was also getting very wet, but he listened, smiling politely, and at the end said goodbye politely, as a young animal should with an old animal. When Dobinson was gone he pressed the button on his new weather-watch.

'Ping Ping Ping rain easing off in the late morning. Good bye,' it said.

The rain was easing off when he reached the beech grove behind Fred and Charlie's cabin. Here he heard loud voices that weren't talking about cricket at all. Two dozen stoats were standing about there, all aproned, most of them looking annoyed, some angry.

One attractive red-haired stoat with a clear voice and a steady gaze was speaking.

'Oh yes, we hear a lot about Kindness in the forest,' she called out.' Stoats shouted agreement.

'Right! Right on! Me too!' And they clapped this good-looking speaker, whose name was Bold Ginger.

The rain had stopped, so the Bottle Rabbit shook himself dry and squeezed his paws dry, and sat down on a dampish beech-stump to hear more. He knew about Ebenezer. He was a second-cousin of Sam the Bear as a matter of fact. ('My grumbling cousin,' Sam always called him. They didn't get on.) Ebenezer ran a big milk business, and all these stoats worked for him, delivering milk, cleaning the milk-cans, and so on.

'I don't like Ebenezer very much,' piped up a tense little stoat called Lollopy Paul, 'Bold Ginger's right. He isn't kind at all. He doesn't even pay me enough for my bread and cheese. My auntie has to pay for half of it every week to help me. And I wheel big heavy milk cans about all day long for Ebenezer.'

Other stoats voiced complaints: up in the dark often, milk-can cleaning all afternoon, often not back home till dark, very bad pay, no time off, no fizzy drinks machine.

Bold Ginger raised a paw high in the air.

'Brothers and sisters I hear you, I hear you. We all agree Ebenezer has been too hard on us. Too hard on us for too long. Surely now is the time. Now is the time to do something about it. All stoats unite! Let us act now to throw off our chains!'

Cheering broke out. But all too soon it was stilled as a bear burst through the trees, a bear in top-hat, morning-coat and black-and-silver striped trousers, smoking a cigar. This was Ebenezer. He was a fairly huge bear, though nothing like as huge as his cousin, Sam. Ebenezer looked different. He lacked Sam's calm, benign air, that note of solid decency and good nature. This bear looked selfish, as he was. He looked untidy, too, with cigar-ash all down the front of his frock-coat, and dents in his grey top-hat, and he scratched himself all the time.

He stared angrily at the stoats, who had gone very quiet.

'Was that a lot of talk I'm hearing here, just now? Is this what I pay you good money for?' Ebenezer's unpleasant voice grew louder. 'Did I hear some stoat, some female stoat, say something had to be done?' he went on, 'Well I'll tell you what has to be done. I want every single stoat out there on their second milk-round, now. It's Monday morning, right? Milk's been delivered, I take it?'

'Oh, yes, Ebenezer, it's all been very carefully given out,' said Woolly Bill, a worried Stoat with a large family.

'So what are we waiting for? Get out there all of you and start collecting my money.' Ebenezer stared round. 'I've got a family to feed too, you know. I don't give my milk away for nothing. So get out there. I've missed breakfast with all this, you know. And I've had enough of this lounging about and talking nonsense.'

Stoats glanced at one another and sadly shrugged their shoulders. They were all trudging off back to work when Bold Ginger in a low fast stoat-whisper said, 'All stoats-dinner-time-one-o'clock-meet-here-all stoats.'

The Bottle Rabbit, now dry, watched the stoats leave and heard what Bold Ginger said. Then he hopped off round to Emily's Tree-home for a cup of tea. But he meant to drop in at the beech grove with Emily at one o'clock for the meeting. It sounded very interesting, though puzzling.

Meanwhile in another part of the forest, Ebenezer's only child, Tim, was playing truant from school, not for the first time. Tim was a nice-looking little bear, very bright, but unfortunately a bit lazy and quite greedy. At this very moment, for instance, he was gulping down honey from a brown pot. It was some of his father's extra-special stock of private honey.

Tim had sneaked it out of the pantry early that morning, in his school-bag. At present he was sheltering from the rain under an ash tree and had a sticky paw deep into the pot. 'Yum, yum,' he murmured happily, and smiled to think of all the other young animals doing algebra, especially Count Hubert. He and Hubert had little scuffling fights all the time at school, but they were also friends in an odd sort of way; they laughed about the same teachers. 'Actually, I wouldn't really mind having old Hubert here now,' Tim thought to himself, smiling.

The young bear was half-way through his honey-pot, feeling happy as can be, and wondering what to do next, when he heard some crackling and whistling in the bushes. 'Hullo, what's that?' he murmured. Then, 'Pooh,' said the bear, 'I expect it's just some jackdaws. Wanting my honey I expect. No chance of that.' And he pawed another sweet mouthful.

Then Tim saw that it wasn't just some jackdaws. Out of the bushes hurtled three masked desperadoes, breathing hoarsely, running fast, holding out a heavy net. Tim goggled at them, sticky mouth wide open.

'You must be those...' he began, but in a trice the desperadoes had their heavy net over Tim's big head and small body.

'Right, Bagot?' grunted the first, bulky desperado. The third desperado, Green, smirked.

'A nice, juicy little prize,' he cackled. It was those same three bad ferrets again, escaped and at their dirty work, and looking nastier than ever.

The little netted bear could hardly move an inch. He lay dumbfounded, until Bushy picked up the half-full honey-pot, grinned, and gobbled it all down with much lip-smacking.

'Not bad at all,' he grunted.

'Greedy beast. That was my honey,' cried Tim.

'Your honey? I bet you pinched it somewhere. I know you young bears. You're all the same.' Tim blushed angrily.

'I don't care. You let me go or I'll tell my Dad about you.'

'Your Dad,' snorted Bagot, 'That Dad of yours will soon be handing over a tidy little sum in coins and notes if he wants to see you again.' Bagot was thumbing about in the honey-pot as he spoke. Then it

104

was Green's turn.

'Oh, yes. Don't worry. We'll be bringing pressure to Bear,' the ferret sniggered.

'You beastly rotters,' shouted Tim, twisting and turning in the heavy net. Though rather lazy and greedy he was also a brave little bear.

'Mallet?' suggested the irritated Green, fingering the one he had hanging at his waist. 'Shall I bop him?'

'Too noisy,' growled Bushy, 'And anyhow, you're a bit too keen on using that mallet, Green. It's my mallet you know. I found it.'

'Took it you mean,' said Bagot.

'Shut up you,' snapped Bushy, and the three ferrets started a fierce quarrel, shouting and scrabbling about. The truth is, none of them trusted one another, especially after that mallet-bop, pill-knock-out business in the badger-girls' aunt's cottage-kitchen on Friday. Now they argued all the time. The kidnapped little bear lay there, trapped in his heavy net but watching them always with his keen eyes.

By now on the other side of the forest the sun was shining in the beech grove. It was well after one o'clock by the Bottle Rabbit's new watch and tired stoats were plodding to their meeting. The rabbit had brought Emily along and the Golden Baker was there, too. He was doing a good business in left-over yesterday's pies, selling them to the badly-paid stoats at half-price. 'Sunday pies! Lovely fresh Sunday pies!' he called out.

Twenty minutes of munching. (The pies in fact were still quite good if you added a dab of mustard or a pickled onion.) Then Bold Ginger sprang up on a beech-log.

'Attention all stoats and stoat-friends,' she cried. 'We are met here to deal with Ebenezer's unkind, or rather unjust behaviour. Now is the time to act. Now!' A great cheer arose.

'Act we should,' called out a fine old stoat named High Gilbert. He wore a much-mended apron and had threadbare gloves on his old paws, but there was something dignified about High Gilbert's straight back and carefully combed whiskers.

'Act we should,' he repeated. 'but surely we must begin in the time-honoured stoat way. We must sing our Marching Song.'

'Hurrah! Hurrah! The Marching Song! Hurrah!' cried out all the stoats, none more lustily than Bold Ginger.

'Very well , then: All Stoats Form Fours,' Cried High Gilbert. The excited creatures quickly moved into six neat groups of four apiece.

'All Stoats as one. March! cried the venerable old animal, and with one more 'Hurrah!' the massed stoats swung into their ancient march. Up-Down, Left-Right, Reverse. Up-Down, Left-Right, Reverse, keeping perfect step across the beech grove.

'Now! All Stoats Sing!' And the Marching Song burst thrillingly from twenty-four stoat-throats:

> Stoats! Stoats! Stoats! Stoats!
> Marching along in our pride.
> Stoats! Stoats! Stoats! Stoats!
> Our courage can not be denied.
>
> Each summer, each winter,
> As temperatures splinter,
> We alter our costumes, but we -
> Stay stoatly, yes stoatly,

So stoatly, all stoatly,
Oh, stoatly and noble and free!

'Next verse!' commanded High Gilbert, and the
stoats thundered it out as they strutted:

Stoats! Stoats! Stoats! Stoats!
Dauntless from cradle to grave.
Stoats! Stoats! Stoats! Stoats!
All handsome and happy and brave.
Each summer, each winter,
As temperatures splinter,
Our fur changes colour, but we -
Stay stoatly, yes stoatly,
So stoatly, all stoatly,
Oh, stoatly and noble and free!

The Bottle Rabbit and Emily, caught up in these
rhythms, couldn't help themselves and swung into the
last rousing chorus, the rabbit hopping up and down as
the stoats wheeled for a final march. The Golden Baker
was grinning and nodding and waving a half-eaten
pie. All roared out the last refrain one more time:

Stay stoatly, yes stoatly,
So stoatly, all stoatly,

Oh, stoatly and noble and free!

Then the animals stopped abruptly, panting and smiling, shook hands all round, and their milk-meeting began.

Bold Ginger took the floor straight away.

'The Action is simple,' she cried. 'No can-cleaning this afternoon, no milk-delivery tomorrow. And... no money collected for Ebenezer.' Excited murmurs all round.

'Then what happens?' called out a stoat with a bicycle.

'Well, there's no one else knows the milk like us. Ebenezer will have to listen to us, and treat us better.'

Cheers broke out. Cries of 'Right On! Stoats Rule!' But Woolly Bill looked worried.

'What if the milk goes sour?' he said.

'Exactly,' cried Bold Ginger. 'That'll show him.' Woolly Bill still looked bothered. 'Excuse me, I'm afraid I see another problem,' said High Gilbert, thoughtfully. 'Our older customers, they really need their milk and some can't get out to get it. We stoats have a duty -'

'They'll take their chance same as everyone else,' called out a thin-lipped stoat at the back; it was Flash Harry, 'Can't make an omelette without breaking eggs.' A few stoats tittered nervously.

'No, no, wait a minute,' said Bold Ginger, pulling at her red hair, 'That wouldn't be stoatly. We'll get them their milk. We'll work something out, do a special delivery just for them.' More cheers. 'But what if Ebenezer locks the dairy doors?' said Woolly Bill.

'Break 'em down. Break 'em down,' cried stoat after stoat, 'Hurrah! Hurrah!' And the Marching Song sprang up again, only to die down as one more doubting voice was heard. It was Dingle Millie's. Everybody liked Dingle Millie.

'Hang on, hang on,' she cried softly. 'Don't forget last time we tried to make a fuss - that business with the rusty milk-cans? When Ebenezer got those terrible ferrets round to bother us in the evenings? Remember Bushy, Bagot and Green coming in and hurting Bald Stanley and poor little Lollopy Paul?'

A bothered silence. Then,

'No problem. No need to worry about those three any more,' shouted a loud non-stoat voice. It was the Golden Baker speaking with great authority. 'The Ferret Board of Trustees has 'em well under control after that badgers' aunt business. They're all day long at work cleaning up the woods - real hard labour. Then back to the Stone Barn at night,' the Baker laughed. 'No visitors. Nothing to eat but cold porridge. They even took away Bushy's leather riding-boots. Don't worry, you won't see those three desperadoes free in the woods for many a day if the Ferret Trustees know anything about it.' He laughed again, rather harshly.

The Golden Baker of course just didn't know what was going on at that very moment in another part of the forest. The very same desperadoes, having cleverly used their ferret-skills to escape from the Stone Barn, now had a prisoner of their own. Their kidnapped victim sat plump and shackled on the grass floor of a secret woodland hut hidden deep in the pinewoods, as the three miscreants plotted new crimes. Bushy, Bagot and Green's nasty plan was to extort plenty of money from Tim's rich father, Ebenezer, and from the Forest Community as a whole. Since their escape the ferrets had gone from outrage to outrage. After dragging Tim here and tying him down, they'd raced off, masked, to rob the grocer's, to steal peppermints and hair oil, and grab the change from his till.

Now they were devouring a late lunch, mostly out of tins. Respectable animals though once they had been, their manners, especially Bushy's, were growing deplorable. The big ferret, for example, was spooning up chunks of tuna straight out of the tin, not even bothering with a plate. He finished his tuna and pawed over the other tins they'd taken.

'Confound it,' he grunted, 'We forgot the baked beans. That's twice. It's your fault Green. I specially told you.' 'Oh for goodness sake shut up about baked beans,' snapped Bagot. 'Baked beans, baked beans... it's all we ever hear. There's lots of other stuff to eat.' Green sniggered but said nothing as he daintily spread smoked goose paté on Bath Olivers. Bushy turned on him:

'Keep quiet, you...'

'I didn't say anything...'

'You sniggered.'

'Who sniggered?' Again the three of them were bickering back and forth.

They got very hot with one another. At one point Bushy held a wide shop-made raspberry tart upside down over Green's head. He was going to squash it all over the smaller ferret, but stopped short when he noticed young Tim grinning in his corner.

'What's so funny?' Bushy grunted, lowering his raspberry tart.

'You ferrets are. All three of you. Squabbling like a lot of School-kids.'

'School-kid yourself,' snarled Bushy, 'I'll teach you. Where's my mallet? Bagot, what have you done with my...?'

'It's not just yours..'

'Yes, it is.'

'Who says?' Yet again the ferrets were at it, and they soon came to blows.

This was exactly what Tim wanted. If he could keep them arguing and fighting like this they'd forget about him, and he might gain some time. And then who knew?

It was tea-time at the beech grove. The stoats were milling about. No can-cleaning had been done.

'Time for a vote on tomorrow's Milk,' called Bold Ginger.

'Quite right,' said High Gilbert. And twenty-four stoats were on the point of voting Yes or No, when with astonishing crashing noises Sam the Bear burst through the trees. It was an extraordinary sight. Sam was heaving and puffing; his eyes glared. His huge black chest was strewn with leaves, even branches, torn off in the speed of his coming. Onto his shoulders clung the badger-girls, looking alarmed. The animals in the beech grove were simply stunned.

Sam scrunched to a stop in the middle of the grove, his great chest heaving.

'There's trouble up the hill. They've escaped,' roared the bear, 'Yes. They're gone.' He sat down on a beech log, panting, then began to speak quietly and firmly.

'Someone must alert Fred and Charlie. And we'll need the Tiger Toms as scouts... Emily, use your influence there. And I'm delighted to see we have the Stoat Group with us. Having a picnic are you? Charming. I know we can count on you stoats for -' He broke off; Emily was holding up a quiet white paw. 'Yes?' said the bear.

'Who's escaped, Sam? We really don't know what

you are talking about.'

'Oh. Yes. Indeed. Yes. In the haste of the moment I... The fact is I have bad news for you all... Believe it or not, those three monstrous ferrets have somehow eluded their captors. Yes. They are once more loose in the forest. Already they have robbed the grocer and the chemist. Yes. And they took a mallet. They are desperate. They will stop at nothing. Already I have collected the badger-girls, for their own safety, after Friday's goings-on at their aunt's cottage. There must now be a grand combined effort to bring these dangerous malefactors back under lock and key.'

The forest animals knew what their duties were. As Sam finished speaking Emily had already slipped away into the woods. The stoats were already planning forest-searches. With low angry mutterings a grim-faced band of ferrets in Trustees' uniforms, all already armed with mallets, strode out from the trees to join in the hunt. Fred and Charlie thundered up, and Pob was somehow there, waving his famous hat.

'Its Moanday. What do you expect?'

Maud the Bear appeared, in heavy leather field-boots, carrying a great basket of meringues. And a distant mewing grew louder and louder until up through the beech trees came streaking the redoubtable Tiger Toms, led by Fergus, with Emily prancing beside him. The Tiger Toms were chanting in their guttural way. They had a new cry,

'Get those cads! Get those cads! Get those cads right now!'

Sam nodded to each new group of arrivals. He had his maps out and was organising. 'It's looking like a lot of work for you night-active stoats,' he was saying to High Gilbert and Bold Ginger. 'And for you badger-girls' when again he was interrupted with the worst news yet.

A frightened squirrel came scurrying. 'Anyone know where Sam the Bear is? Oh, there you are. Thank my stars. I have a message for you. It's from three really horrible ferrets.'

Dead silence struck the beech grove.

'They told me I had to bring a message to you and a message to Ebenezer, or they'd bop me with their mallet. They were horrible. I've already done Ebenezer.' The squirrel was shaking from head to foot.

'Yes. Now. Calm down and hand me your message my dear fellow,' said Sam, 'You're safe now.' He nodded to the badger-girls. 'Margaret, Dorothy, give him a bun and some lemonade, or milk; there's plenty of milk. Now let's see what this message is all about.' He took a piece of crumpled paper from the frightened squirrel, smoothed it out, and put on his enormous spectacles. As he read the message, the bear shook his

113

huge head and looked very stern.

'Yes. Much as I might have expected. The ruffians.' He shook his head again. Animals grew impatient.

'Read it out Sam,' everybody shouted, 'Sam. Please read out the message.'

'Yes. Yes, of course. It runs: "We've got Tim. There's nothing you can do. You'll never find us. If you want Tim back send us twenty-five pounds each, that's three lots of twenty-five. Also a dozen tins of baked beans. Also a new tin-opener, ours is bent. Also a keg of beer. Signed: Ferret Power. P.S. We've got a mallet."'

Groans from many animals, and cries of horror from the group of Ferret Trustees.

'Preposterous,' said Sam, 'If Ebenezer got the same note as this, that's three times twenty-five plus three times twenty-five; that's, er -'

'One hundred and fifty pounds,' said the Golden Baker.'

'And two dozen tins of baked beans,' added Dorothy.

'Not to mention the beer,' said Fred, 'and two tin-openers.'

'Preposterous,' said Sam again, 'And of course there's no knowing whether they'd free poor Tim. How awful. Tim's a touch idle and inclined to greed, I think we'd all agree. But at heart he's a good little bear.'

Animals called things out:

'Splendid young bear.'

'Really decent bear.'

'Good old Tim,' echoed from all sides. There were some sobs.

'Tim good old friend' said Pob.

'How did Tim's father take the news, Mervyn?' Emily asked the squirrel-messenger. Mervyn, after his bun and lemonade, seemed much calmer.

'He's terribly upset, is Ebenezer,' he said, shaking his head, 'I left him at his dairy, sitting on a dirty milk-can just staring.' Stoats flinched. He kept saying "Poor Tim. Poor Tim." I think he was crying. He's a changed bear.' Animals shuddered and looked at one another.

Sam cleared his throat, 'Don't worry. We shall catch these miscreants and rescue Tim. And don't worry, not a single penny will they get from us, not a single baked bean.' The Ferret Trustees gave a roar of approval. Maud, who'd been re-reading the crumpled message, looked up with a deep sigh.

'Sam,' she said gently, 'We couldn't pay them if we wanted to. The stupid creatures forgot to tell us where to send the ransom.' In spite of herself she gave a little laugh, and soon, awful though things were, so did everybody else, and the whole beech grove echoed with quiet mirth. Meringues were handed round from Maud's wide basket and everything somehow seemed a little easier.

At this point Sam clapped a paw to his brow. 'Good gracious. What have I been thinking of all this time? Bottle Rabbit. Are you there? Yes, of course you are. Good. And you have your bottle with you I'm sure? Good. Tonight you must pongle as you've never pongled before. Yes. We shall need all the forces at our command.'

The Bottle Rabbit stood up, blinking shyly as he felt all eyes on him. 'We'll leave the details of your pongling to you, my dear fellow,' went on Sam, 'I think you know best what your Magic Bottle is capable of.' Animals cheered up even more as the rabbit modestly hopped off into a corner and settled down to what was to be the greatest pongling session ever held so far.

Where to start? That was his first thought. Perhaps a

few sandwiches? No, no. There was urgent work to be done and he began straight off with the General Alarum. He took a deep breath: 'Pongle-Pongle-Pongle-Pongle-Pongle-Pongle-Pongle.' In a flash the Golden Eagle was there on the ground beside him. As evening was drawing on, the noble bird's extraordinary eyes (they could see 1,000 miles in any direction from high up) could not be immediately useful. But all knew that when dawn came on Tuesday those eyes would be sweeping the forest in the most intense way imaginable.

The Bottle Rabbit took another deep breath, then, 'Pongle-Pongle-Pongle-Pongle,' and 'Pongle-Pongle-Pongle-Pongle-Pongle.' In no time at all the pleasant jingling of bridle and reins and the tuneful hooting of a posthorn announced the arrival of the Mouse Carriage. Up trotted eleven oversized, powerful-looking white mice, pulling behind them a bouncing finely-carved ivory state-carriage with spangling wheel-spokes flashing. Nigel, as ever in elegant uniform, spun his posthorn in one gloved paw. 'Evening all,' he sang out, 'And a very special good evening to you,' he added in an aside to the Bottle Rabbit, 'Some animals needing transport somewhere, sir?'

Nigel was interrupted by the roar overhead of a blue-and-white aeroplane. The Six Blue Hares were responding to their pongles and preparing to land. Minutes later they bounded up in their brightly-plumed shakos:

> 'Yes, sir.'
> 'Yes, sir.'
> 'Yes, sir.'
> 'Yes, sir.'

116

'Yes, sir.'

'Yes, sir, where to, sir?'

After all these arrivals it was no great surprise when a high voice was heard demanding, 'What can those absurd ferrets be thinking of? I mean, what are they up to?' It was Norman the Pigeon, brilliant in scarlet blouse, long baggy shorts, and low black boots. He was clearly well over his mumps.

Never had there been such a great assembly of forest animals poised to rescue one of their friends. Sam had his maps out again, and was marshalling his forces for the Great Search. But every animal knew that, apart from some scouting by night creatures like the badger-girls, the massed cats, the stoats, and the ferrets them-selves, little could be done for poor kidnapped Tim until Tuesday morning's sun rose.

It was very dark now, with no moon. Emily had slipped away into the night with the Tiger Toms, and the Bottle Rabbit thought it best to go quietly off to bed, to be ready for the next day. But as he lay by the fireside in the cart-horses' cabin, finishing off a last mug of Charlie's creamy cocoa (the two great Clydesdales had also come quietly home), he kept on thinking about poor young Tim alone, cold and hungry, off in the forest with the three terrible ferrets. How different all this was, he thought, from Sunday's three-pongle world, with its thrones and shows and those obliging antelopes. He snuggled down and yawned and wondered about the stoats - he really liked Bold Ginger - and about how they all had to work so hard with the milk-cans and about Ebenezer being unkind to them and about the milk going sour in the morning and about Flash Harry's thin lips and about Mervyn wait a minute who was Mervyn again and he yawned puzzledly and tried a little night-cricket scoring a few runs in his private half-asleep way and yawned more and more and slowly drifted off into a troubled sort of full sleep.

Rescue, and a Feast

The air was stale in the bad ferrets' hut at seven in the morning. Tins of half-eaten corned beef and spam lay about, glasses half-full of beer stood on tea chests. The three desperadoes shifted and creaked on their mouldering sofas. They were waking up.

'What are you going to spend the money on Green?' mumbled Bagot, yawning and stretching. 'I'm not sure; books and records I expect, perhaps some travel,' muttered Green. Then he sniggered, 'And what about you, Bushy?' ('I bet you it's going to be beer and baked beans' he said under his breath to Bagot). 'Mind your own business. I'll buy what I like, when I like,' shouted Bushy, who had heard him. 'Only asking,' bleated Green. 'Well don't be a nosey Parker. You're nothing special you know. Just because you've had a bank job.' 'Oh for goodness sake shut up, you two,' shouted Bagot. 'And who asked you to stick your ugly nose in?' shouted Green. And so their morning began as their evening had ended.

Young Tim sat shackled and cramped, listening to their pointless noise. The small bear was tired and terribly hungry. He'd missed breakfast again. Indeed he'd only had one bowl of cold porridge since Monday morning. But the brave young animal could still manage to smile to himself. He was thinking that if he could egg the ferrets on to make enough of a row, some kinder animals might sometime hear it, get there and somehow rescue him.

In another part of the forest a very different kind of noise, a busy clinking and clanking, had been going on since five that morning. The stoats, after some debate - for how those stoats loved their meetings - had decided to hurry back, clean the milk cans and deliver Tuesday's milk at highest possible speed before joining the Great Search for Tim. The Twelve Mice were helping them. It was a strange sight, the delicately carved state-carriage crammed with jangling milk cans, stoats running and jumping behind it. More oozing cans were strapped on top of the coach, steadied in place by the big mouse, Nigel, who was enjoying himself. 'Milk-o. Here comes the milk,' he would cry, and then give a tootle on his posthorn. Norman the Pigeon flipped and flapped above. Meanwhile, as stoats raced from home to home with their cans and bottles, the Blue Hares buzzed overhead on the first of their spy-missions over the forest.

The stoats were doing the milk mostly to cheer up Ebenezer. 'I don't get it. I just don't get it,' Flash Harry

kept complaining. 'Just when we've got the boss over a barrel.' But the stoat-group had found Ebenezer sitting on a milk can, staring into the trees, tears rolling down his big bear's face. 'Poor Tim,' he kept saying over and over, 'Poor Tim.' The animal didn't seem to have any idea what to do next. So they got him to sit on a newly cleaned can, left him some breakfast, finished their jobs, and tore back to the beech grove, where Sam was already at work organising search-parties for the little kidnapped bear.

Messages kept coming in as the morning wore on, from the Golden Eagle, from Emily and Fergus, from the badger-girls, from the Trustees, from all the great army of friendly animals spreading through the forest, searching and searching. But the night-patrols had found nothing and no good news had come yet today.

———

'So when do you think the money's coming, and the beans?' asked Tim quietly from his hut-corner, towards noon. 'Shouldn't be long now,' growled Bushy. 'They've had all last night and all this morning to collect it. Anyhow, shut up, you.' The three ferrets were taking lunch, out of tins again. They'd been eating for a long time, but had given nothing to Tim, whose little bear's stomach was rumbling. 'It'd better come soon,' said Green, slinking over and prodding Tim in the rumbling stomach. 'Or you'll be fading away, lazy, greedy little bear that you are.' Green sniggered.

Tim was hungry and frightened, but he kept calm. He had a plan.

'Where are they supposed to bring it then?' he asked in the same quiet voice.

'What do you mean, where? Where we said.' Green was beginning to look uneasy.

'Well, where did you say?' Tim persisted. The ferrets wheeled and stared at one another, knitting their brows. Then they all started shouting at once.

'It's your fault.'

'Fault yourself.'

'You didn't put an address.'

'No more did you.'

'Stupid idiot.'

'Stupid oyt.'

'Horrible fat pig.'

'Cheap little biscuit-eating faker.'

'Half-ferret!

'Half-ferret!' Each loudly taunted the others with this supreme ferret insult, and immediately a battle-royal was raging, the worst yet. Tins went clattering across the floor, hurled plates cracked on the hardwood walls, bottles broke and splattered, flung chairs splintered. Green got first to the mallet, and, his narrow snout working, flung it at Bushy, who ducked. Crash it went through the window, just as Bagot sent Tim's father's empty honey-pot - crash! - through another. Pandemonium reigned. Exactly what Tim had hoped for. 'Now is the time, now is the time,' he told himself. And 'Help!' he shouted as loud as he could. 'Help me!' The ferrets took no notice as they shoved, pushed, kicked and yelled at one another.

'Help!' shouted Tim again and again.

And help was not far away.

Stoats have remarkable ears. Like the massed cats and the Ferret Trustees, they'd been given a section of the forest to search by Sam. They'd gone over it inch by inch, almost, but try as they would they'd seen nothing.

Stopping for a breather they were looking at one another unhappily, when suddenly forty-eight stoat-ears pricked up. The clamour from the distant hut had dimly reached them.

High Gilbert held up a paw in command. 'All stoats in platoons,' he cried. Then, 'Stoats-at-the-double. Quick march.' They didn't just march; not another word was spoken as three groups of eight stoats sped off through the forest, heading towards the unmistake-able crash of shattered glass and falling masonry, the growling hubbub of bellowed insults, and - yes - the heart-breaking voice of a small bear crying:

'Help me! Help me!'

Bold Ginger, brave and undaunted, raced head up at full speed, leading her platoon as they burst through thick foliage and reached the hidden hut-door. At that very moment the shadow of the Golden Eagle passed over their heads. The news would soon be general over the Forest. Stoats bunched at the hut-door.

'All stoats heave!' from High Gilbert, and eight of them put their backs to the door with hoarse cries of 'Ut Hoy! Stoats Hoy!'

They broke its hinges, stumbling backwards into the midst of the on-going battle. Stoats and more stoats poured into the hut, falling over one another, scuffling and scrambling. It was a maelstrom. Often enough stoat punched stoat as they struggled excitedly to subdue the bruised and battered ferrets who bit and snapped and bit again. Bold Ginger at last had Green cornered and caught, while Woolly Bill and Lollopy Paul, of all people, pounced on Bagot and, with another cry of 'Ut Hoy!' stilled his dangerous claws. At last even Bushy, growling and spitting, was a prisoner too, heaving under the weight of three strong young animals. 'All stoats halt!' called High Gilbert, standing beside the sink at the back of the secret hut, and a moment's panting silence followed.

'Here, handle this vile creature would you?' Bold Ginger summoned two members of her platoon, thrusting Green into their ready paws.

'It's all Bushy's fault,' snivelled the frightened ferret. Then the attractive stoat slipped over to little Tim's corner and, with her can-cleaner's pliers, snapped the manacles off the young bear's wrists and ankles. Tim scrambled up smiling.

'Thank you very much Bold Ginger,' he said as he rubbed his stiff limbs. 'Gosh. I'm really hungry.' And he padded over towards a scattered heap of tins. 'Bother, the opener's bent,' he said.

As the stoats smiled on Tim there was a commotion. Bushy was fat and strong and cunning.

'Aargh!' With a triumphant howl he twisted and turned his heavy body, bowled over his three captors and made like a bullet for the gaping doorway.

'Aaargh!' again, and out into the underbush, up-ending Flash Harry on the way; Flash Harry, who'd lingered out there, not too keen on the fighting. Big brutal Bushy charged on clear of the bushes, trumpeting yet another 'Aaargh!' as he got out into the open.

But this one died away as he stopped dead and looked all around him.

Fiercely gleaming through the leaves on the left of the clearing were the eyes of all the ranged Tiger Toms, with Fergus crouched panther-like in front of them, his long tail swinging and swinging; Emily bristled at his side. Above the low-slung cats, two Clydesdales stared down deep into the fat ferret's eyes. Bushy looked

desperately to the right, only to find row upon row of
Ferret Trustees with fixed snarls on their faces and
raised mallets in their paws. The Golden Eagle had
done his work well. Last but not least, straight ahead of
Bushy towered Sam the Bear, black and huge; beside
him Maud, standing resolute in her flowered summer
hat; beside her, a blinking Bottle Rabbit. And a blue-
and-white plane buzzed close above the doomed
ferret's head.

'It's a fair cop, dearie,' sang out a high voice. Norman
the pigeon of course, popping about in the back-
ground. Bushy stood blankly still, chest heaving, a
terrible scowl on his battered, wobbling snout. He now
had no hope. He had nowhere to turn.

Young Tim skipped out through the hut-door, palefaced, but safe and well, swallowing cocktail sausages as fast as he could. A great cheer went up; the forest animals had reclaimed their own.

With cries and whimpers Bagot and Green came tumbling roughly out of the hut; then even Bushy trembled as the Trustees moved in with their mallets.

———

All the ferrets disappeared into a dark part of the forest, dragging the three desperadoes with them in a painful procession. The Trustees growled in grim chorus as they went, 'Urgh. Urgh. Urgh. Urgh. Urgh.' A frightening, rather horrible sound, but it was a very happy procession that wound its way back with Tim to the beech grove to meet Ebenezer. Pob had been telling the worried bear about how everybody shared things out in the township of Yes. 'Ever body happy.' Ebenezer had seemed quite interested.

Tim ran straight to his father and the little bear, who'd been so brave for so long, now burst into tears. 'Daddy, oh Daddy, I'm sorry I took your special honey, Daddy,' he sobbed. 'I'll never do it again. And I promise I'll try and be better at algebra.' Ebenezer flung his paws round the small bear and hugged him. Then father and son went off to one side for a while and sat quietly together under a tree.

A whole new feeling was in the forest now. Celebration was in the air. The sun shone in the beech grove. Animals began setting up tables, bringing chairs, making a platform for music, decorating the trees with bright banners and coloured lanterns. A Great Forest Feast was being prepared, mostly by Maud and the Golden Baker, but with many assistants. There was much laughing and singing.

'What'll happen to those awful ferrets?' the Bottle Rabbit asked Emily as they were carrying out a large tray of Maud's meringues together. The rabbit had his new dark green jumper on. A bit long, but nice. 'What'll they do to them? Will they hurt them?' he asked anxiously. 'Only a bit, I should think, said Emily. The Bottle Rabbit shuddered. 'With mallets?' he asked. 'Oh, I doubt it, ' Emily coughed delicately. 'They're having a special Trustees Meeting about it now. I expect we'll hear this evening.' She went on, 'Sam's been advising them. I'm sure they'll do the right thing.'

The stoats were resting in a group after their heavy morning. Many had bruises. Some of them even had bandages on from the hut-fight. Sam and Ebenezer and Tim moved over to greet them, Ebenezer raising his arms high in the air. By now his frock-coat was torn and milk-stained, and his top-hat had no crown to it, yet there was a new dignity about this bear.

'How can I thank you all enough, dear stoats? Dear brave stoats? What can I possibly do to show my deep gratitude?' Ebenezer rested one big paw on little Tim's head. Stoats looked embarrassed, hung their heads, muttered things like 'Only doing what had to be done.' 'Did what any animal would do.' 'The pleasure's ours.' But Bold Ginger raised her head and fixed the bear with her clear eyes. She was going to speak out, when Sam said, 'I believe I can help you, Cousin Eb. Come with me.' And the two bears plodded off, paws over shoulders, back into the forest for a long friendly talk.

The cousins had at last become friends.

Meanwhile, Tim and Count Hubert had met and were laughing and chattering together. The Bottle Rabbit couldn't help overhearing them.

'Lucky you, getting off school yesterday,' said Count Hubert. 'Pooh,' said the little bear, 'I bet you wouldn't have wanted to be tied up by that fat, smelly old Bushy instead.' Count Hubert sighed.

'We had algebra; I hate it; there's no counting at all. And guess what? Pongo fell asleep in class.'

'He did?'

'Yes, right next to me, nearly fell off the bench.'

'Old Blaggers must have gone bonkers' said Tim.

'Oh, Blaggers did one of his "Sit up straight, fold your arms and listen" things.'

'Wagons and stars?' asked Tim, smiling.

'Yes. 'Hitch your wagon to a star, boys and girls.'

'Sorry I missed that.'

'Yes. And the best part was that Pongo fell asleep again.'

'Brilliant,' said Tim.

'Blaggers didn't think so,' said Count Hubert. 'He gave us all three extra problems to do, just for laughing at Pongo. We didn't get out for ages.'

'Good. Serves you right.' The two young animals giggled and punched one another, scuffled, and then ran off laughing under the trees. Tim was himself again.

———

Sam and Ebenezer ambled back from the forest, Sam smiling, Ebenezer looking pleased with himself.

'Good news,' cried Sam. 'We have a special

announcement for all stoats.' To everybody's surprise, Ebenezer now kicked his feet in the air and did a little jig.

'I am as light as a feather. I am happy as an angel, I am as merry as a schoolboy,' he cried to the wondering stoats. Ebenezer skipped and leapt again. 'Everything's going to be different for everybody from now on,' he crowed. 'And I'm giving up cigars. I'll start tomorrow.' And off he skipped, puffing on an extra long one. 'I am as light as a feather,' he cried again, to the trees.

The stoats crowded round Sam.

'What's he on about?' 'What announcement?' 'Why's he skipping?' Sam smiled.

'It's about your jobs. My cousin is so grateful about Tim, he is going to double everyone's pay.' 'Hurrah!' from the stoats.

'He is cutting down work-time.' 'Hurrah!'

'There will be a free hot lunch every working day.' 'Hurrah!'

'He is going to work on the can-cleaning himself.' 'Hurrah!'

'And from now on he will be wearing an apron like everybody else.' 'Hurrah! Hurrah!'

Stoats danced and clapped. A 'Stoats! Stoats! Stoats! Stoats!' broke out and was sung right through.

When it was done Flash Harry raised his narrow head,

'No fizzy-drinks machine, then?'

'Fizzy drinks?' said Sam. 'I beg your pardon? Oh. Yes. The drinks. A small oversight. Bear with me, and I shall get back to him about the drinks. I am sure he will agree. Yes.' Other stoats laughed at Flash Harry, chaffed him, and sang a good deal.

All afternoon the happy preparations went on. Marvellous smells began to drift across the grove. The tables groaned with fishes and meats, cheeses and fruits, breads, buns, cakes and pies. One special table held a collection of the Bottle Rabbit's own special sandwiches. In mid-afternoon he'd pongled up a good number of them with his Magic Bottle, also quite a lot of lemonade. At tea-time, a long limousine rolled up with four poodles in the back seat and three beagles in the front. Bard, Berm and Burt, carrying picnic baskets, hurried over to help Maud and the Golden Baker, while the poodles lounged in the limo, sipping their malt whisky.

Almost everybody you could think of was in the beech grove by now. All the usual animals, of course, but Hamish MacPie had dropped in, also some foreign dachshunds off a ship. Fred's Aunt Norah came, and the ant, Maurice, with his brother Albert. Other guests were Ralph and Lloyd, the labrador umpires, the Paris cats, Phillipe and Josette, Basil the thinking owl, down from his home at Mimic Hootings, and the quiet mouse-chemist from his nearby shop. Howard and Trevor, the bulldog policemen, were there in their brown suits, and the two Clydesdales Fred and Charlie had invited the ferret accountant Baxter in a spirit of forgiveness. 'Bushy?' he'd said, when asked about his fellow-ferret, 'I wash my paws of him.' Baxter had come with his sister Aggie, a pretty little smiling creature. And even Airedale Jack had run down from the North with a brown paper parcel of baps and barmcakes, specially baked by Maisie. Late in the evening a group of handsome antelopes turned up.

At seven o'clock, loud honking and piping and drumming came clattering through the trees. 'Ranald's here!' cried Dorothy excitedly. 'I can hear him.' She blushed. 'I mean it's the Booge People. They're coming!' And there they soon were, down from the hills with their wheeled instruments, small and hairy and happy as they blew and plucked and beat on bassoons, basset horns, bagpipes, bass fiddles, bass drums, bongos and bones. Pob was waving his polished hat.

'Is going to be a good long party,' he said. 'And by the way, in township of Yes weeks begin on Tuesday.. not Wednesday. The badger-girls nodded agreement.

Just as the really serious munching and gulping was getting under way, one more group of friends arrived. Margaret held a paw to her ear.

'Hark,' she said, 'Listen. There's some more animals singing.' And sure enough, through the summer evening trees, above the clink of plate and glass, the happy chatter and the honks and plucks of Booges tuning their instruments, sounded the words of another stirring song:

> Knees, knees, glorious knees,
> Make up a parcel of buffaloes' knees...

Could it be? Yes, it was. Out from the forest burst a singing, prancing troupe of armadillos, dressed in their circus best. Daisy was there, brilliant in lime-green, waving her favourite sequined handbag. Fred, looking pleased, strolled over to greet her with a mug of cold beer each. A long chat began. The Booge Music broke out and with a roar of delight, the forest animals leapt up and danced.

Sam was resting after his first vigorous jig when, to his surprise, Egbert, the ferret Trustees' Secretary, slipped out of the woods and spoke quietly to him for some time. Sam nodded his head solemnly as Egbert slipped away again, glancing longingly at the Great Feast as he went. The mighty bear now padded over to his rabbit friend, looking serious.

'Bottle Rabbit, I've been speaking with Egbert. You should be the first to know the news. Yes. It's Banishment for those three. A heavy sentence indeed.'

'What's banishment?' asked the Bottle Rabbit, his mouth still full of buttered bap.

'It means Bushy, Bagot and Green will never be back. Yes. The hopeless word of "Never to return." A hard thing for an animal to leave his homeland forever; but it can't be helped, it has to be done.'

'Where'll they go?'

'To Polecat Hall, a big training school miles and miles away in the West Country. They'll be taught better ways there; then off with them to the West

Woods for hard work. They will be kept busy and out of trouble, you may be sure.'

'They will have homes though?' asked the anxious rabbit.

'Oh yes. Once they have learned to behave like normal decent ferrets they will have their own little places. But after all their badness, they are banished from the forest for ever. Exiled.'

'What's exiled?'

'The same thing.' The Bottle Rabbit shuddered.

Now Sam clapped his paws for general attention. He had been planning to make a very long speech about all this and about Ebenezer's gift of a full set of croquet balls, hoops and mallets to the Foresters' Cricket Club and about related matters. But just at that very instant, the Booge People burst into a new loud rhythmic ball-room-number. Animals leapt to their feet and the Grove was filled with whirling couples. Sam was taken aback for a moment, then shrugged his massive shoulders, smiled, put a paw out to his wife, Maud, and the two huge bears thundered contentedly off into a foxtrot.

The Bottle Rabbit could only do one sort of dancing, the hopping up and down kind, so he mostly wandered about, munching a bit and then gulping a bit, chatting to animals, listening to animals chatter. He came among the stoats again.

'What are you going to spend your extra money on?' Lollopy Paul was asking High Gilbert.

'I think a new apron, to start with,' said the dignified old animal.

'I'm getting a present for my auntie,' said Lollopy Paul.

'What a kind and generous bear Ebenezer has turned

out to be,' cried Woolly Bill. 'Lots more money, no more getting up in the dark, a fizzy-drinks machine.' Bold Ginger's clear voice interrupted him.

'Well, I'm pleased of course. But it's not so much kindness we're talking about, is it?' She stood up, slim and attractive. 'Ebenezer's only doing what's right, after all. You know, we could have made him do it - our way - with the milk cans.' Bold Ginger looked firm and strong as she said this.

'Right on,' murmured some stoats. High Gilbert gave her a quiet smile and half-nod, half-shake of his head. The Bottle Rabbit looked at her, admiring, but puzzled.

More and more animals were dancing. Stoats had started up their own odd high-speed bobbings about, and lithe Tiger Toms were everywhere. Nigel and Norman were doing a double-quick joke-dance, knees high, paws waving, wings fluttering. Norman's voice came shrilly over the music,

'Nigel, really! That's my foot you keep standing on, Nigel. And me in my best Doc Martens. Shame on you!' On they danced.

Now the Bottle Rabbit was talking to Fred, who was drinking another quiet beer with Daisy.

'You know, Fred, I sort of wish Ken was here. He'd love this.' Fred drained his beer-mug and pointed with it across the Grove.

'He is here. Do you see that person in a Spanish cape near the food tables? The one with sandwiches in both paws - both trotters, I should say? It's Ken; he's in disguise again.' Fred was pointing at a big animal with false nose and moustache, glossy wig and dark green spectacles. Poised in front of him was a goat in a business-suit with a briefcase, holding up sheaves of paper and reading things out from them. The larger animal was staring about and didn't seem to be listening much.

'It's him all right; it's Ken,' said the Bottle Rabbit. 'I'm going to try to talk to him. And I think I know that goat. He's -

The rabbit broke off as the big pig came hurtling over on tip-toe, making twinkling pirouettes as he came. Ken had always been good at pirouettes. With one trotter cupped behind an ear, he sang in an amusing fluting voice:

> Don't get me wrong,
> For I'm rarely to blame.
> But did some little dickie-bird
> Tweetle my name?

The Bottle Rabbit looked round for a dickie-bird. The pig shook his head and rolled his eyes.

'Come on, Bottle Rabbit. It's me, old man. It's me... it's Ken.' He slapped the rabbit on the back.

'Oh, hullo Ken. I hardly recognised you. I haven't seen you all week, not since last Wednesday; are you having a nice time?'

'I'm very glad you asked me that question, old man. I'm having a super time. Smashing.' Ken lowered his voice. 'See that old goat over there?'

'Yes,' said the Bottle Rabbit, 'as a matter of fact I -' But Ken swept on, 'He wants me to publish a huge long poem of his. It's about an old warrior rabbit, he says. I think he's going to pay me loads of money to do it before he's finished. I'll be able to pay off that confounded beaver, even.'

'Oh, Ken, really.'

'No. Not what you think, old man. All honest and above-board, old man, cross my heart.' Ken grinned and winked.

Booge music struck up again, and the rabbit was swept away from Ken by surging crowds of dancers. He looked round for Emily. She'd had several dances with wild Fergus, prince of the Tiger Toms, he'd noticed; now he was happy to see her reclining on a beech log. So he hopped carefully round to it and plumped down beside the beautiful white cat.

'Hullo, Bottle Rabbit. Isn't it nice to see Fred and Daisy dancing together again? It is such fun, dancing in the Beech Grove.' Emily stretched her long white cat-body and looked over her shoulder at him.

'Yes, I know,' said the rabbit, 'But there's some important things I wanted to talk to you about.' He took a deep breath.

'I mean about the last seven days, this whole week since last Wednesday. Everything seemed simpler before. At Fred and Charlie's cabin and everything. I mean I know lots of nice things have happened this week. Hubert and his bike, and us in the water-meadow, and the cricket, and Sunday, and Tim getting saved today, and the stoats, and the Feast. But there've been so many puzzles, Ken for instance. I mean I do really like Ken, but he does try to cheat animals, doesn't he? And I think he's doing it again now, with that goat poet we once met. Then there's poor Hubert; he loves his new bicycle almost as much as he loves counting, but why did Howard and Trevor have to be so horrible with him? And then be really kind and save us from the bad ferrets the very next day? The cricket was lovely, but I was worried all the time, and they called me a horse, and stoats bet on me, and you know my winning shot was a bit weird. Sunday was lovely all day... perhaps we should try to stay for always in

that three-pongle place? I mean, bad things began
again here on Monday, the ferrets worse than ever with
poor Tim. And now they are banished. It's horrible.
And then Ebenezer. At first he was horrible, and then
he got unhorrible, and he's being very kind to the
stoats, now. But Bold Ginger I really like bold Ginger,
and she looks so nice, too. Bold Ginger says Ebenezer's
not being specially kind, he's just doing the right thing.
It's all so... so puzzling. What do you think, Emily?'
The Bottle Rabbit trailed off, shaking his kind rabbit's
head after this, the longest speech of his whole life. He
fingered his Magic Bottle.

'Do you think she's all that good-looking?' asked
Emily. The rabbit glanced at the cat. 'Well I... well, yes,
she is... for a Stoat.' Then he glanced at Emily again and
leapt up. The Booges had started one of their throbbing
specials, the kind even he could dance to. He held out
a paw.

'Emily. Let's dance this one, please let's.'

Emily leapt up at once, smiling her startlingly beautiful white cat smile, and off they went, a charming
pair. The rabbit hopped hard and happily, his Magic
bottle popping about in his pocket; Emily slid smoothly
in step. All around them hopped other happy animals
lost in the pounding Booge Music.

'I think I'm going to forget all about three-ponglers
for now,' the beaming rabbit thought to himself, 'I like
it here, and I've always got my Magic Bottle, and
there's all sorts of other perfectly good pongles
possible.' Emily now grinned her cat-grin at him and
straight away everything seemed to be all right after all
most of the time in this friendly world of forest
animals.

No animal went to bed at all on that happy night in

the forest. There were songs, there were stories, there were jokes, there was more gulping and munching, there was much, much more music and dancing. And it all went on and on for Emily and the Bottle Rabbit, just as it did for all their forest friends, far into late Tuesday night and on into early Wednesday morning, when, happy and sleepy, blinking in the new sunlight, they saw that it was time for breakfast. Nobody was going to miss that. And already a whole new week had begun.

The End

Also available

BOTTLE RABBIT

The Bottle Rabbit won his Magic Bottle as a Kindness Prize, and when he pongles it properly, very good things appear: lovely sandwiches and ice-cold lemonade, a private moose-drawn luxury coach, or even a private plane. But bad animals like the Crad and the Grumble try to steal the Bottle, sometimes in very frightening ways. However, with the help of his good Forest friends, the beautiful white cat Emily, Sam the Bear (huge, black), and Fred and Charlie, the two great Clydesdales, things work out in the end.

With Axel Scheffler's witty drawings.

'A racy and most original piece of fancy'
Margery Fisher, Growing Point

'The Bottle Rabbit stands out in this age of over-packaged books for children by retaining a strong sense of its original identity...'
The Observer

'A real find'
Books for Keeps

Shortlisted for *The Guardian*'s annual Children's Books Prize, 1988.
Published by Faber & Faber. Now available from Merlin Unwin Books, Palmers House, 7 Corve Street, Ludlow, Shropshire SY8 1DB. **£4.95** paperback

BOTTLE RABBIT & FRIENDS

Some villains are after that Magic Bottle: a concealed rat, a cat named Raoul, two sinister sheep... and the Grumble strikes again. But Bottle Rabbit's friends are there to help, as always: Emily , Sam the Bear, Fred and Charlie. New friends also appear, Daisy the dexterous Armadillo, little Pob with his edible furniture, the hairy, musical Booge People. Ken the Pig dodges in and out, as unreliable as ever.

With more of Axel Scheffler's inspired illustrations.

'The dialogue is vivid and convincing, the descriptive writing dense and poetic, and the stories are so tuneful that they deserve to be read aloud to your very dearest friends'
The Guardian

'Marvellous'
Books For Your Children

Published by Faber & Faber.
Now available from Merlin Unwin Books, Palmers House, 7 Corve Street, Ludlow, Shropshire SY8 1DB.

£4.95 paperback